MW00769475

Two Degrees
One Heart

Acts 20:35

June Enjoy &
relax & let love
read you to Two Degrees
One Heart.

de de
Cox
10/6/19

de de Cox

Copyright © 2019 by de de Cox

TWO DEGREES ONE HEART

All rights reserved. No part of this publication may be reproduced, distributed, or transmitted in any form or by any means, including photocopying, recording, or other electronic or mechanical methods, without the prior written permission of the publisher, except in the case of brief quotations embodied in critical reviews and certain other noncommercial uses permitted by copyright law. For permission requests, write to the publisher, addressed "Attention: Permissions Coordinator," at info@beyondpublishing.net

Quantity sales special discounts are available on quantity purchases by corporations, associations, and others. For details, contact the publisher at the address above.

Orders by U.S. trade bookstores and wholesalers. Email info@ BeyondPublishing.net

The Beyond Publishing Speakers Bureau can bring authors to your live event. For more information or to book an event contact the Beyond Publishing Speakers Bureau speak@BeyondPublishing.net

The Author can be reached directly BeyondPublishing.net/AuthordedeCox

Manufactured and printed in the United States of America distributed globally by BeyondPublishing.net

BEYOND
PUBLISHING

New York | Los Angeles | London | Sydney

ISBN: 978-1-949873-39-9

DEDICATION

There are so many to thank and never enough space. My best friend, my sports lover, my partner, my hoarder of drum kits and bulldogs, my husband, Scott, don't ever stop arguing with me or sharing that sense of humor. My sister, Casonya, you inspired me. Were it not for you and growing up with you, this dream would not have become reality. To my two boys, Isaiah Bo and Matt – I am and will forever be your biggest cheerleader and support. To my momma, Linda – who always shakes her head because she cannot keep up – thank you for being my Mom. Eileen and Shelly, you guys support me and my ideas for who I am. You never judge. You both are there with words of encouragement. Logan "my Logie" – you are the daughter I never had. Marietta, thank you for always listening. Rebecca, remember, you have my ending. To the good Lord – when you spoke the words of Isaiah 40:31 – there are no truer words than to wait upon You and Your perfect timing.

"This book has what we've all daydreamed about... the possibility of a chance meeting in the most unusual of places - an elevator. Two Degrees is a story within a story. An intriguing romance full of excitement that only a medical drama can bring. You wont be disappointed!" – **Eileen**

Two Degrees
One Heart

Sometimes when you wake up, you just know "it's gonna be one of those days." That's how Gracie Lynn felt as she pulled into the parking lot; an uneasy feeling had been with her since she woke up. She thought to herself, she was grateful for her job, she loved her job, she loved her co-workers - BUT more, she loved the children. So, without glancing back, she opened the car door and entered into her haven – the Pioneer Children's Hospital.

Inside the hospital, it smelled like cotton candy. Gracie had no idea how the hospital made it always smell like something soft, something pink (her favorite color), and something so comforting. It was like magic.

It took Gracie back to when she was younger and in high school, when graduation had been just around the corner. Her friends had all been thinking about summer break and their first year of college in the fall. Gracie had graduated with honors from her high school. She was popular, but not popular. She had friends, but not close friends. Her circle consisted of three (Logan, Arie, and Landon). They were best friends and shared a lot. All had met in middle school and continued their friendship through high school. Gracie was close to Arie and Landon.

Logan was a different matter. He was athletic. He played every sport. He was smart. He was her confidante. But the most endearing quality of Logan Gere, he was kind. Gracie knew it. Gracie had thought and had hoped the relationship would develop. As the years progressed, she gave up hope for a romantic relationship. Instead, Logan and Gracie had remained best friends. When one was sad, the other was there with a shoulder to lean on or cry on. It was more Gracie needing the shoulder. Logan was always there.

School was Gracie's "pink" cloud. She was smart, she was intelligent, and she was what some would call "cute". She was comfortable in her surroundings. She had never been referred to as pretty. All the comments were, "She's so cute." It never bothered Gracie, because she was confident in who she was.

And, so, the day had come, graduation. It was finally here. After the ceremony, Logan, Arie, and Landon met. Family and relatives were hugging and congratulating the graduates. Then, it was time for Logan and Gracie to hug. Logan walked towards her, and Gracie knew this moment was important. She watched him as he grew closer. Suddenly, she felt as if the world was closing in. Her knees began to shake, and she could not speak. Not one word. What was going on? This was just Logan—or was it "just" Logan? Logan grabbed her hand and began to rub the inside. Gracie felt she could not talk. Logan looked into her eyes and touched the side of her face with his other hand. Her face turned towards his palm. What was wrong with her? Something was about to happen, and Gracie did not know if she could stand upright. Logan looked at Gracie intently and whispered ever so lightly in her ear, "Thank you, thank you for being my friend. Thank you for being there. But mostly, thank you for being you". Logan took a breath in. Gracie took a breath in. It was just the two of them (Arie and Landon were not there). In that moment, Gracie knew. She was in love with Logan. Yes, she loved him, but after all these years, she was in love with him. And it was too late.

When did Gracie get on the elevator? Had she been sleepwalking from the car into the hospital? Was she rude to anyone while walking in?

Did she forget to say hello to her superiors? Goodness, how did she get in the elevator? Well, it didn't matter. She was ready to start the day.

Gracie had gone to college and had pursued her BSN. She loved children growing up, and she loved them even more in her career. It was five years of intensive study, but she did it. She had interviewed at so many hospitals. Finally, Pioneer Children's Hospital in Denver, Colorado had called. An interview was set up. As soon as she walked in, she knew this was the one. State-of-the-art research and state-of-the-art technology to help fight childhood illnesses and diseases – Pioneer Children's Hospital was number one. Gracie felt blessed.

As her co-workers were getting on and off of the elevator, she felt excited to start the day. Every child who was admitted to Pioneer Children's Hospital held a special spot in Gracie's heart. The job was too easy. All Gracie needed to do was show kindness, caring, and compassion – referred to as the Three Cs by her grandmother. Gracie remembered her grandmother telling her to always show the Three Cs. When her grandmother told her what they were the first time, Gracie had looked at her, perplexed, because "kindness" did not start with a "c". Her grandmother looked at Gracie and said, "You are correct, but I have captured your attention, and that's what you are to do with the Three Cs." Gracie never forgot that conversation and always remembered to practice the Three Cs. Gracie thought to herself, *Sometimes, it's the smallest of things that have the biggest impact.* A word, a gesture, a compliment, or a hug, Gracie knew the children needed it—and her, as well.

She repeated the Three Cs to herself in the elevator, *Kindness, caring, and compassion.* Then, it happened, everyone was in a rush and the elevator was filling up rather quickly. The elevator would not hold one more person, no way – but it did, because a hand slid in and the doors opened again to add another, and it was *him.* It was quite early.

Gracie stood in the back of the elevator and caught herself moving to the corner. She did not want him to see her. Could it be *him*? No, her eyes were playing tricks on her. A couple of more times, Gracie peeked around a co-worker's shoulder on the elevator, just to be doubly certain it was *not* him. Her heart was racing. She could actually feel it beating through her scrubs. Could anyone else see her heart beating? Did anyone else know what was going through her mind? Could they read her thoughts? Before Gracie could confirm that it was *him* – he had stepped off the elevator, onto the fifth floor. Gracie's floor was the seventh. She tried her best to get a good look, but it was impossible. She thought to herself, *It was just the light. Yes, just the light.* He could not be in the same hospital as she was. He was dressed in scrubs, just like she was. He could not be a pediatric nurse, just like she was. This was too much. Where was the seventh floor? Why was it taking so long?

Finally, her floor. She was safe. She was in her environment. She was okay. As Gracie approached her desk and computer, she could not help but feel that this day was going to be different.

As she began her rounds to check in on her patients, Anna approached her and asked if she was okay. "You are looking a little flush, Gracie," she commented. Gracie was thankful for Anna. Gracie had met Anna in nursing school. Both graduated with their BSNs. Both loved children and were happy to be at Pioneer Children's Hospital. Both had become fast and best friends while in nursing school.

Gracie replied, "I'm okay, just a little flustered this morning." Gracie told Anna she thought she had seen a familiar face from high school, but that it had probably just been the lighting in the elevator.

Anna told Gracie, "If you need anything, just let me know." Gracie was so glad Anna was in her life. Again, Gracie had kept to herself in nursing school. Anna was the opposite of Gracie. Anna loved dining, movies, and dancing. Gracie loved reading and writing. Gracie was thankful that Anna was the total opposite. Gracie was thankful that Anna was the friend she had become - Gracie's best friend. Anna never judged Gracie, but always kept an open mind. Anna always had the attention; whereas, Gracie hid in the background and observed. Again, it wasn't that Gracie did not want the attention. It was the fact that Gracie never sought the attention. Her studies and career had become the focal point in her life. There was no time for boyfriends or even *a* boyfriend.

Gracie had had several love interests, but never that one defining moment that said, "Wow, it's him. This is the one. This is the one who I can share my life with forever. This is my soulmate." Such feelings were foreign to Gracie. She had only experienced the emotion of love once. That had been a long time ago. Life moves on. Different adventures, different individuals, different characters coming into your life. Some, Gracie would consider just acquaintances.

Gracie looked at Anna and said, "Okay, here we go, let's get the day started." Gracie and Anna separated and headed down the hallway to their assignment. What would the day hold?

As Gracie began her rounds, she could not get the thought out of her mind, *Was it him?* She had to stay focused. She couldn't continue to daydream. Her first patient was a beautiful five-year-old little girl, named Sarah. Sarah had been diagnosed with the beginning stages of leukemia. Sarah had been admitted early this morning to begin her first round of chemotherapy. Gracie knew that the first time was always the scariest, so she knew she would need to pull out the magic to make Sarah feel safe. Gracie also knew that not just informing the parent, but also informing the patient of what was to take place was very helpful. Knowledge is education. Education is knowledge.

As Gracie was about to open the door, she heard a small giggle. Was that Sarah's laughter? She did not want to disturb Sarah if her parents were helping her to prepare for what was to take place. So, before she knocked to interrupt, Gracie listened to his voice that told Sarah, "Pick one." Then, she heard, "Place it back in the deck. Don't tell me, I'm going to find your card." That voice. That masculine, deep voice. A shiver went down Gracie's spine. No, that could *not* be the same voice. The same sensual voice from long ago. A voice she thought she would never hear again.

His voice said, "Now, remember your card." Gracie heard Sarah's little giggle again.

Sarah replied, "Okay, I know it."

Gracie could hear the placement of the cards on the little table. Then, she heard his voice, "Sarah, I need your help. You must think really hard about your card. Concentrate on the card you chose." A moment later, she heard him ask, "Is this your card?" Gracie heard a little squeal of excitement from Sarah, which fell into place with his voice – it was him!!!

It was Logan. It *had to be* Logan. There was no mistake. She remembered his voice. Gracie remembered the deepness of his voice. She remembered the sensuality of his voice that day so long ago.

She heard his voice say, "Okay, now, let's get you ready for your first day of chemotherapy with us. Don't worry, I will be here when you get back, and we will do another magic card trick." Gracie heard Sarah's small, tiny voice say, "Thank you," and, then, she heard the parents thank him.

Before Gracie could pull away from the door, the door began to open.

12

She could not move. Her feet were in concrete. Her feet were in glue. Her feet were stuck. Logan had his hand on the door. What was Gracie to do?

Quickly, she turned around and walked briskly to the next patient who needed to be seen. She was out of breath. She was going to pass out. She needed a wall to lean up against. Gracie's heart was pounding so loud she could see it. She was inside the room of her next patient, and the young man's eyes were bigger than saucers, because Gracie could not breathe. Noah was her next patient. She did not want to scare him. She calmly took a breath and turned around.

She said, "Good morning, Noah."

Noah looked at her and asked, "Miss Gracie, are you okay?" He added, "You are really pale. Please come sit down with me."

This was her patient telling her to sit down. It should be the other way around. Gracie looked at Noah and said, "Thank you."

Noah was ten years old. He had been playing basketball early in the morning with his older brothers and had suffered a minor concussion. He was in Pioneer Children's Hospital for an MRI. Gracie asked, "So, how is your morning going?"

Noah looked at her as if to say, "I am okay, but what about you?" Gracie had to chuckle a bit. She went over and began to do the vitals on Noah. Blood pressure, heart rate, pupils, questions about nausea and dizziness.

"So far, so good," she told Noah. "Our next step is the MRI." Gracie told Noah he had taken quite a hit on the head when he had fallen on the driveway. Gracie had Noah sit straight up in the bed, so as to view the small knot on the back of his head. Gracie reviewed the checklist—measurements, swelling, and tenderness. Noah told her that his mom had just left to run and grab a quick snack and drink. Gracie knew that Noah's mom probably needed to collect herself. Gracie knew that look. Once the patient had been registered, checked in, and confirmed for a room, and all was well with their child, the parent needed that moment just to recollect themselves before the next step. Gracie had seen that being a parent was not for the lighthearted. It was serious business. It was a job. It was 24/7. There were no breaks in between. Gracie thought to herself, *I want to be a mom. I want children.* For the moment, though, her full attention was given to Noah.

On the other side of the door, Logan could not believe it. He had just left Sarah's room and was getting ready to visit the next patient, when he heard her voice. Her voice was talking to Noah, the young man who had been admitted for a concussion while playing basketball with his brothers. Logan did not want to or mean to eavesdrop—it had just happened. He could hear her voice tell Noah what she was doing and why she was doing the check-off list. But he had also heard Noah ask, "Miss Gracie, are you okay?" Logan only knew of one Gracie. This was his Gracie from high school. Was it her? Could it be? The chances of both of them being in the same hospital, the same floor, the same career– Logan's mind was going fast and furious with all the what-ifs and could-it-bes. Logan was impressed with the questions "Miss Gracie" was asking. Logan had suffered a concussion from football as a teen in high school. One that had almost ended his career. So, Logan knew firsthand what his coach and doctor had asked him. Yes, "Miss Gracie" was covering all the "needed" questions. Her voice was soft. Her voice was tender. Her voice was caring. Just as he remembered from high school. Logan needed to get to his next patient. This was his first week at Pioneer Children's Hospital. He did not need to be daydreaming. Logan thought to himself, *I will need to find out if "Miss Gracie" is **my** Gracie.*

And, so, the day began. Rounds and checking on the patients. Most of the patients ranged in ages from five years old to twelve years old. The ages where anything *can* happen and typically *does* happen. Logan thought to himself that this was the age when everyone became a daredevil. This was the age when the children were no longer babies and not yet teens, but maturing. This was the age of sports and cheerleading. He thought, *This was a great age to be when I was a kid.*

Gracie finished with Noah. She signed the paperwork, and out the door she went, to begin the next follow-up. Gracie knew with the summer, the floor would be full of "accidents" and "spills".

Gracie had finished her last patient for the morning. She knew Anna would be finishing as well. They both had agreed to meet for lunch in the hospital cafeteria. Even though hospital cafeterias don't have a good reputation for food, the cafeteria at Pioneer did have good food. It provided a well-balanced meal, with a large selection to choose from. Gracie's stomach had been in knots since the morning encounter of the voice—she knew it could not be his voice. As she was wondering to herself, Anna bumped into her.

"Are you okay, Gracie?" she asked. "You seem like you are in a daze. Did anything happen today with one of your children?". The nurses at Pioneer Children's Hospital always called the patients "their children". Gracie had several patients who had been with her for one to two years, due to their illnesses. Sometimes, they would leave and come back and, then, other times, they would not leave. These were the children who tugged at Gracie's heart. Gracie kept a list of those children. She wanted to remember why she was doing what she was doing.

As Gracie heard Anna's voice, Gracie said, "Yes, I'm okay. Just heard a voice from the past."

Anna looked at Gracie. This was not like Gracie. She looked a little flush. A little pink around her cheeks. Anna was going to keep a close watch on Gracie today.

Anna looked at her and said, "Let's go get something before our break for lunch gets away from us." Gracie agreed and approached the line.

What would she have? What was she hungry for? Gracie knew what she was hungry for. She was hungry for his voice. She was hungry for his touch. She was hungry for his hand to gently touch her face one more time. She wanted to feel his hands everywhere on her. She was hungry to feel the caress of his hands in places that he had not touched the entire time she had known him. Gracie thought to herself, *What am I thinking? It's not him. How **could** it be?*

As Gracie and Anna were reviewing what they were going to have for lunch, Gracie got an uneasy feeling in the pit of her stomach. Working in a pediatric unit, nurses were always catching what the children caught, but this did not have the makings of being sick. Gracie ordered her favorite sandwich, chips, a drink, and dessert. Dessert was her favorite. Chocolate chip cookies were her downfall. Gracie turned around to see if Anna was finished ordering her lunch.

As she turned, Gracie saw him. He had just walked through the cafeteria doors as though he owned the cafeteria. It was Logan. Time could not pass any slower than it was at this very moment. Gracie felt as though everything was frozen in motion. Logan's walk was one with a purpose. He gazed on the food with anticipation. His smile was inviting.

Goodness, where did Anna go? Gracie thought. She went ahead through the line to check out. She did not want to stay behind. She did not want to wait for Anna. She had had a very rough morning, and it probably showed. Gracie could not see Anna anywhere. Approaching the cashier, Gracie went to get her money to pay. A quarter dropped on the floor. Gracie knelt down to reach for the quarter, and at the same time, a hand connected with hers, and she dropped the quarter again. Gracie stood up, and Logan opened the palm of her hand, gently laying the quarter with a small sweep of his fingers.

Logan whispered to Gracie, "You dropped something."

Gracie thought to herself, *I sure did. My heart just dropped.* She managed to say the words, "Thank you, Logan."

Logan looked deeply in her eyes and said, "It's all my pleasure. Let me know if you need me to pick up anything else?"

Gracie stumbled with the words, "No, I'm okay. I think I only dropped the quarter."

Logan had his hands free from placing his tray down to help Gracie and decided at that very instant that Gracie needed direction. Logan placed both his hands on Gracie's waist and gently turned her towards the cashier and whispered from behind her neck, "Your turn".

Gracie was caught off guard. *My turn? My turn for what? Oh yes, to pay. Good lord, I'm falling apart over a quarter.*

Gracie paid and began to walk through the line. Gracie did not turn around. Gracie did not want to know where Logan was sitting for lunch. She did not want to know if he was following her. Gracie needed to get far away.

Then, she heard Anna's voice say, "Hey, aren't you the new nurse on the pediatric floor?" Who was Anna speaking to? It was not Logan. It could not be Logan. It was Logan.

Gracie then heard Anna say, "Please come join my friend and me."

Could this day get any more stressful?

Anna hollered for Gracie to turn around and come join her and her new friend, Logan Gere. Gracie did not want to join Anna. Gracie did not want to sit with Logan and eat food. Especially in front of Logan. But Gracie knew Anna would not take no for an answer, so she turned around and walked towards the table where Anna and Logan were seated. Anna had placed their wallets, badges, and other necessary items in the chair beside Anna. That meant that Gracie was going to have to sit beside Logan. Gracie looked at Logan.

He patted the chair beside him and said, "Please sit beside me, I won't bite."

Gracie immediately felt a flush come to her cheeks. "Nibble" was more the word that came to her mind than "bite". What did she want Logan to nibble? Gracie's mind started flooding with ideas. Possibly, gently nibble her lower ear. What about the lower lip? Logan could nibble that. What would the nibble feel like on the base of her neck or the small of her back? What would happen if the nibble travelled a bit lower? Gracie felt it. It was in her heart. She felt an ache for something in her breasts.

Logan patted the chair again for her to sit beside him. She snapped out of the daydream and sat down. Anna and Logan began to eat. In between bites, they were discussing the day and the children who had been admitted. Gracie could not eat. She was too consumed by the man who sat beside her. The man who exuded the scent of masculinity. The man who exuded sex as soon as he walked into the room. The man who could melt a thousand hearts as soon he looked at you with those baby blues. Gracie would be losing a lot of weight this summer if eating lunch with Logan continued.

Gracie listened intently as Anna asked Logan a lot of questions about himself, his education, his career, and his overall intent with nursing. Logan responded with the normal answers. He was from a small town. He had graduated high school and immediately left for college to pursue his nursing degree. He had then applied for employment at some of the most prestigious children's hospitals. When he had interviewed with Pioneer, Logan had known this was the hospital for him. He wanted to pursue becoming a traveling nurse. He had one more year at a children's hospital and, then, he would be able to apply for travel. Gracie liked what she had heard. He had a goal and was on track to accomplish his dreams.

As Gracie went to take another bite, she felt Logan's leg brush up against hers. Mind you, scrubs are not the most attractive item of clothing, nor the softest, but she felt the brush all the way to her inner thigh. A slight shiver escaped Gracie. Logan looked at her and asked if she was okay. Was the cafeteria too cool? Gracie wanted to say, "Did you just brush your leg against my leg?"

All she could muster was, "I'm okay, just a bit cool."

Gracie did not want to tell Logan that she was actually feeling hot. She was feeling hot near her inner thigh. She was feeling hot in regions that should not be feeling hot. Gracie thought, *I am too young to have hot flashes, so it could be a virus.* Gracie knew it was not a hot flash. Gracie knew what it was. It was Logan. It was Logan, her friend from high school, who had Gracie feeling hot.

She needed to escape. Gracie needed to get back to her floor. She had patients to check on. Gracie made the motion to stand, and before she could say anything, Logan stood up and pulled the chair out for her. That one gesture made the biggest impression on Gracie. He was a gentleman. He had manners.

Logan looked at Anna and said, "I guess I better be going, too. I need to check in on a few of the kids I looked at this morning." No, he didn't. That meant that both of them would be going in the elevator, riding up the elevator together to their assigned floors. Anna told Gracie she would be up in a few minutes. Gracie thought, **Now** *you are lagging behind?* Most of the time, Anna was in a rush to get back on the floor. But today, she chose to stay behind. Really? Really?

Logan gently touched the small of Gracie's elbow and said, "Let's take our trays through the line and get ready to go back." Her entire body was shaking. Gracie did not know if she could hold the tray while Logan was holding her. Gracie nodded in agreement.

As they approached the elevator, Gracie asked which floor Logan had been assigned to. The seventh floor.

Phew, that was close, Gracie thought. Gracie was the fifth floor. The elevator doors opened, and Logan motioned for Gracie to go first. As Gracie walked in, Logan was right behind her. Gracie wondered to herself where the other thousands of hospital employees could be. *Is no one else going back to work on their assigned floor?* It was just her and Logan.

Gracie took a deep breath in and turned around to face the elevator doors, but when she did, she did not realize how close Logan had become. His face was too close. She inhaled his scent. Logan had a distinct scent. It was warm. It was masculine. It was sexy.

Then, she heard his voice whisper ever so lightly, like a feather on the inside of your arm, "You look the same still, my Gracie. Still beautiful."

Gracie could not look up. She could not look into those big, beautiful baby blue eyes. It was like drowning in a pool of cool water. Logan gently put his finger under Gracie's chin and kissed her on the forehead and said, "It's your floor. You *are* the fifth floor, correct?"

Yes, I am the fifth floor, Gracie thought. *Where are the words?* All Gracie could do was nod her head in agreement and exit the elevator. As she exited, Gracie turned around. Logan was smiling as the door closed. *Good grief, what is going on with me? It's only mid-day, and I'm a wreck. Like as in semi-trailer wreck.*

Gracie began to walk back to her desk to prepare for rounds. More than likely, she would not see Logan again. Possibly, she would not see Logan until the morning when they both arrived for work.

The afternoon went by fast. So many children. So many illnesses. Gracie was tired. Anna had sent a text informing Gracie to wait for her by Gracie's car before leaving for home. As Gracie was walking to the parking lot, she felt good. Gracie loved children. But she loved making the children feel safe and secure in an environment that could sometimes be rather big, scary, cold, and uninviting. Gracie's steps were deliberate. Walk to the vehicle, meet Anna and go home. As she approached her car, she saw Logan and Anna deep in conversation. Why was Anna speaking with Logan? What interests did she have with Logan? She could hear their laughter. Why were they laughing? What were they laughing about?

When she was close enough, Anna squealed with delight, "You didn't tell me you knew Logan." Gracie wanted to say, "And how do *you* know Logan?" Anna was a little too close to Logan for Gracie's liking. Gracie pulled her keys out of her tote and nudged her way between Logan and Anna in an attempt to open her car door. As Gracie was ready to open the door, Logan placed his hand on top of Gracie's to open the door as well. Gracie said thank you and got in. Gracie was ready to close the door when Anna reminded her of their dinner date tonight at their favorite sushi restaurant. Gracie had forgotten. It was Logan's fault. Gracie was not prepared for what came next.

"Oh, and by the way, Logan is joining us," stated Anna, as a matter of fact.

NNNNNNOOOOO, Gracie thought. *This was our girls' night. He is being intrusive.* Logan was simply smiling down at her with a look of triumph. Gracie wanted to wipe that smile off his face. There was an uneasy feeling coming over Gracie with Logan so close.

He leaned in and whispered, so Anna would not hear, "Would you like me to come?" Okay, that one word had multiple meanings. Meanings that were blocking her mind with thoughts of Logan.

Shaking her head, Gracie told Logan, "No, it's fine, you can come." Logan chuckled and smiled his incredible grin from ear to ear. *Oh my lord, what did I just say?* thought Gracie. Gracie could not believe she just said that. She needed to drive. Drive to the restaurant and gather her thoughts.

Logan leaned near, so only Gracie could hear, and said, "Okay, I'll come, if that's what you desire." Now, this was getting out of hand, actually hysterical. Gracie pushed his arm away, a little too fast, looked at Anna across the parking lot, and said, "I'll meet you both there." As Gracie was putting on her seatbelt, she watched as Logan and Anna got in their own cars. Good, Logan was not riding with Anna. Now, why that bothered Gracie, she did not know. She just knew all were driving their respective cars. All would separately arrive.

On the drive there, Gracie allowed her thoughts to reflect on Logan. He was tall. He was athletic. His blond hair was now shoulder-length. Gracie could tell that he was physically fit. His arms were muscular. He had a light tan. His smile was still charming. He was sexy in high school, and was still sexy—that had not changed.

One thing *had* changed, though. Gracie had changed. She no longer was a romantic. Gracie was a realist. She had dated one or two guys. Nothing serious. After one date, Gracie's interest waned, and her education and career took the place of any type of intimacy she may have been yearning for in a relationship. Gracie wondered if Logan had had any type of personal relationships. Of course, he did. Look at him.

Gracie approached the restaurant, parked, and sat there. She didn't understand why, but she was apprehensive to get out of her car.

Good lawd, it's going to be all three of us, Gracie thought. She opened the door and walked to the entrance. Logan and Anna were already inside, waiting for her. How long had Logan been there with Anna? What had they been discussing? Why was Anna so close to Logan's shoulder? *Snap out of it, Gracie*, she thought. *Logan is **not** my boyfriend. Logan is **not** Anna's boyfriend.*

When Gracie entered, Logan was there to open the door for her. He immediately placed his hand on the small of her back. This one small gesture placed a smile on Gracie's face. It was an act of kindness. It was the simpliest gesture.

Logan looked at Gracie and asked, "Are you ready?" She was ready. Gracie was ready for Logan to kiss her. To kiss her so passionately that

Gracie would need to feel the strength of his arms holding her, so she would not fall.

The waitress escorted Gracie, Anna, and Logan to their seats. It was a booth. Who was going to slide in first, and who would be sitting with the "other" one? Logan made the decision very easily. He gently touched Gracie's elbow and guided her in the booth and then sat down beside her—very close beside her. Anna took the other side. As Logan slid in, his leg swept against Gracie's. Gracie took a breath in.

Logan looked at her and asked, "Is everything okay?"

No, Gracie thought. *Everything is **not** okay. You are too close. Too close for comfort.*

Instead, Gracie's replied, "Of course everything is okay." Gracie and Anna began to look at their menus. Logan did as well. Their orders were taken and their drinks were delivered. The chatting began.

Anna told Logan of a fundraising gala event that would benefit the hospital. Anna asked if Logan had any plans to attend. Logan looked at Anna and said, "It all depends on Gracie."

Gracie turned around with an astonished look on her face and asked Logan, "What do you mean, it all depends on me?"

Logan replied, "I was going to ask you to attend with me. You know, as my date."

Gracie stammered, trying to come up with an excuse not to attend with Logan, when Anna chimed in, "Gracie probably won't go. She never attends events like this."

Gracie finally replied, "Of course, I would love to go." Gracie could tell Anna was surprised by her acceptance.

Logan was smiling and commented, "That would be great. I'll pick you up at your place at six o'clock sharp."

Gracie nodded in agreement, and the date was set.

When the food arrived, Gracie did not know if she would be able to eat in front of Logan. Her stomach was in knots, just thinking about the weekend and the fundraiser gala. What would she wear? Did she have anything to wear? How would she do her hair? Did she have shoes to match the gown she did not have? Gracie did not have anything. A mad shopping spree was about to take place. Small talk finished out the dinner, and the waitress came by to ask if anyone would like dessert.

Logan reached for his napkin and, like the wind on a cool night, touched Gracie's hand. Chills went up Gracie's spine.

Logan noticed and asked, "Cold?"

"No," Gracie replied.

Logan smiled and proceeded to take the napkin to wipe his mouth. His lips. The corners of his lips. The smile on his lips. Gracie was thinking how those lips would taste. Would Logan's lips be soft and tender? Would Logan's lips be firm and masculine?

Lord, I need to get home, Gracie thought. She needed to be in her home. Safe and secure and away from these thoughts and the man causing these thoughts: Logan. Gracie definitely did not need dessert.

Logan informed the waitress that the meal was incredible and that he needed the check.

Anna said, "That's okay, I can pay for mine." Gracie informed Logan she could, as well. But he insisted and paid for all three.

As they were leaving, Anna was walking in front of them, and again, Logan placed his hand on the small of Gracie's back. His touch was like fire. It went from the small of Gracie's back down to her most intimate parts. Gracie thought she would have to stop and stand still for a moment, just to catch her balance.

When the three friends neared their cars, Logan opened the door for Anna and told her to be safe on the drive home. Anna began pulling away, and Logan looked at Gracie, all ready to head home. Did Logan mean he was heading home with Anna? That was not going to happen. Not in a million years.

Gracie caught herself saying, "Absolutely."

Logan began to guide Gracie to her car, and just as Gracie was about to open the door, Logan placed his hand on top of Gracie's and said, "I'll get that".

And then it happened. It happened quickly and fervently. Logan was moving closer to Gracie. He kissed her gently in the middle of her forehead. Gracie leaned into the kiss.

Logan proceeded to move down towards the tip of her nose and, then, he gently breathed a slight whisper into Gracie's ear, "Thank you."

Gracie melted. Her legs felt like jello. She was going to pass out. She shivered. Logan felt her reaction.

Gracie heard Logan ask her, Are you ready to go?"

Gracie wanted to answer, *Yes, I will go with you*, but the words would not come. She just nodded her head slightly.

The door opened, and Logan said, "Let's get you home." Logan watched has Gracie fumbled with the seatbelt and finally placed it over her shoulders. As he turned and was walking away, he looked back to see Gracie leaning on the steering wheel, shaking her head back and forth.

Logan thought to himself, *That will teach her.* Logan knew what he wanted. Logan wanted her. From the depths of his soul, Logan wanted to feel Gracie's lips caught in a deep, heated, smothering kiss – the kind that takes your breath away, the kind you know must stop sometime, but you cannot stop, no matter how hard you try. Logan wanted to look deep into Gracie's eyes and see the need and want he felt. He was sure Gracie felt the same way. Time would tell.

As Gracie pulled into the driveway of her small cottage home, she needed just a moment to gather her wits. *Goodness, what's wrong with me?*

She felt as if she had a fever. That's it. She was coming down with something. Being around the children all day, germs were passed back and forth.

Gracie opened the door of her car and walked up the steps to her home. She needed to get in there quickly, into her own environment, her safety net. As she opened the door, favorite smells enveloped her senses – her home was tiny compared to some of her friends, but everything had a place and was where it needed to be – familiarity is what Gracie desired this evening. Gracie had left apples on the side of the counter.

She could smell their country flavor. That morning, she had cooked a quick breakfast of bacon and oatmeal – the breakfast of nurses – quick, easy, and fast. Gracie loved her home. It was hers. This was her haven. This was where, for the moment, all was as it should be: quiet and peaceful. Gracie went to the kitchen and opened the refrigerator looking for something sweet. Gracie needed dessert. Nothing looked appealing. Nothing seemed to satisfy her craving. It was a cool, fall evening. Gracie needed to clear her thoughts.

She remembered there was a bakery just up the street. She had visited it when she had first moved to town. It was cozy and quaint. Just what Gracie needed. She changed into her favorite sweats with her favorite long sleeve t-shirt. Yes, this felt good.

Gracie grabbed her wallet, and out the door she went. The bakery was just two blocks away. Gracie approached the shop and noticed there were familiar faces from her street. This was a family place. It was warm and inviting.

Gracie grabbed the handle of the door when a familiar voice said, "Let me get that for you." Gracie turned towards the voice. It was him. It was Logan. What was he doing at "her" shop?

Logan looked at Gracie and said, "I'm out for a little walk." Gracie nodded. She could not speak. All of sudden, she had too many clothes covering her. Gracie felt hot again. It was a fever, it just *had* to be. Logan opened the door and said, "After you."

Gracie walked in. Logan looked at Gracie and said "I've passed by here several times. I heard about this little shop at work, and thought I would try it out. What would you recommend?"

It took Gracie a moment to realize he had asked her a question. Gracie was noticing Logan's attire. It looked as if Logan had just completed a run. Just a bit of sweat trickled down the side of his neck. He wore a very tight-fitting athletic shirt, which was showing off his muscles. Logan had on his sweats, but they were much tighter on him than Gracie's sweats were on her.

Logan looked at Gracie again. "Do you have a favorite cookie?" Gracie nodded and cleared her throat and told him the chocolate chip cookies were to die for. Logan looked at the items on display and said, "We'll take two, please." The owner nodded, smiled, and handed them their treats.

Logan gently took Gracie's elbow and guided her to the table. "Let's sit here," he motioned. Gracie sat down and knew she would never be able to eat the cookie or probably even take a bite. Why was she nervous? Why was she hot? Why was this "feeling" coming over her? Logan began to eat, and all Gracie could do was watch Logan.

Logan looked at Gracie and said, "Do you like the view? You've been staring at me since we sat down."

Gracie looked at Logan and said, "I'm sorry." Logan replied, "No, it's okay. I like how you are looking at me." Gracie's cheeks began to turn red. She was blushing. Logan gently reached for Gracie's hands and began to softly caress the underside of Gracie's fingers.

It's so gentle and soothing, Gracie thought to herself. Instinctively, Gracie's fingers intertwined with Logan's. It was natural.

Logan looked at Gracie and said, "Let's take a walk outside. It's an evening full of surprises."

Gracie looked at her cookie. She was no longer hungry for the cookie. She was hungry for Logan's touch. Gracie needed Logan to touch not just her hands, but her entire being. Gracie nodded in agreement. Both Gracie and Logan said their goodbyes to the shop's owners.

Logan directed Gracie in the direction of her home. Gracie stopped in her tracks. "Logan, do you know where I live?" Gracie asked, concerned.

"No, I know you, and you would not venture far from your home. Just let me know which direction we need to walk in.

Gracie took a step and told Logan, "Just a few blocks." Logan placed the palm of his hand in the small of Gracie's back. She could feel him – oh yes, she could feel him. She wanted to feel him in other ways. As they walked, Gracie could feel a need she had never felt before.

The walk home was in silence. As if Logan knew what Gracie's thoughts were and was allowing her these moments. As they approached Gracie's home, Gracie quickly turned into Logan, in order to cease his movements. She gratefully thanked Logan for walking her home.

She began to walk towards the steps leading up to her porch, but Logan reached for her and said, "Let's sit outside, on the porch steps."

Gracie nodded in agreement, and they both sat. Logan's leg was placed very close to Gracie's hand. For some reason, she felt the need to place her hand on top of Logan's leg. He intertwined his fingers with hers to hold her hand gently to his.

He turned towards Gracie and said, "Close your eyes." Gracie shook her head no. "Yes, Gracie, close your eyes," Logan whispered.

Gracie bit her bottom lip. Not in fear, but in anticipation of what would happen, should she actually close her eyes. Gracie closed her eyes and waited. She felt Logan's hand leave hers and gently felt his hand move up the side of her neck and then he ran his thumb over her lips, like the touch of felt when you rub it between your fingers. Logan leaned into Gracie. She inhaled his masculine scent. Then, it happened – Logan kissed her.

As Logan looked at Gracie, he knew he wanted her, he needed to taste her, to feel her warm, supple body against his. The sweats definitely needed to be removed, and the quicker the better. Logan could taste the sweetness of Gracie's lips. He gently moved his lips over Gracie's. They were soft and moist. Gracie's lips opened to accept Logan. Logan began to swirl his tongue around Gracie's.

Gracie was timid at first, unsure of what to do next, when it just happened. Gracie's tongue betrayed her and did things that Gracie had no idea a small muscle like a tongue could do. The kiss became more passionate when Gracie responded by leaning into Logan. A small breath escaped Gracie's lips.

Logan took one hand and placed it lightly behind Gracie's neck and began to massage the small of her neck – all while still ravishing Gracie with his tongue. Logan's other hand moved to Gracie's waist. His hand slid underneath Gracie's shirt and moved gently toward the cup of her breast.

Gracie felt warm to the touch. Her body was soft. Her breast was supple. As Logan moved his thumb over her breast, he could feel Gracie responding. Gracie wanted him. There was no denying the heat, the passion, nor the need. Logan's hand moved to the back of Gracie's bra and with one snap, Logan had access to Gracie's warm breast. He massaged Gracie's back and, then, moved his hand to feel Gracie's nipple grow hard under his caress.

At that moment, Logan could not stand it any longer. He placed his hand on Gracie's elbow to help her stand and said, "Let's go inside. It's a bit cool on the porch, and I think we may be giving the neighbors a bit of entertainment for the night."

When Logan said "let's go inside", Gracie awoke from her slumber of passion and need.

Goodness, what am I doing? Gracie thought. *Who saw the shenanigans on the front porch?*

"No, you can't, Logan," she replied breathlessly.

Logan looked at Gracie and smiled and said, "Yes, we can. I know you are feeling what I am feeling."

"Feeling and acting on are two different things," Gracie told Logan.

Gracie stood up and placed both her hands on Logan's chest to prevent him from moving one step closer to her front door. Logan took his thumb and placed it on Gracie's lips and rubbed it across her bottom lip. Gracie's lips were soft and pouty.

"Are you sure, Gracie? This is what you want?" Logan made Gracie look at him.

Gracie nodded yes. She then looked at Logan, thanked him for a wonderful evening, and kissed him on the side of his cheek. Gracie turned to unlock the door. She knew it. She felt it. Logan was still on the porch. Logan placed his hand on the door where Gracie was inserting the key and slowly took Gracie's hand off the doorknob. Logan told Gracie to look at him. She turned around and looked directly into Logan's eyes. The intensity, the passion, the need – Logan could sense and see it all, in just that one look.

Logan leaned into Gracie and whispered in her ear, "As you desire, Gracie – I'll see you in the morning at work." And so slowly it seemed like it was in slow motion on a movie, Logan turned and walked down the porch steps. Gracie looked up and watched as he walked back in the direction of the bakery.

Don't look at him, Gracie kept telling herself. *Don't look up. Don't let him see how much you wanted him.* Gracie couldn't help herself. She looked at Logan. He was looking back at her and smiling. This was too much.

What was Gracie doing to herself? To be romantically involved with Logan would not be good for their work relationship. Gracie heard Logan whistling to himself and she unlocked the door and walked into her home. Her warm, inviting home – and lonely. For the first time since moving in, Gracie felt all alone.

Gracie woke the next morning. She felt different this morning. This was the weekend. She had a day off – which rarely ever happened. She was warm under the covers. When she had gone to bed, she needed comfort and had put her favorite flannel pj's on. They were bright pink and purple – just the colors to match her mood this morning. She threw the blanket back, because that was the best way to start the day. She allowed the coolness of the room to make her aware of her surroundings.

Gracie looked over at the clock. It was almost 9:00 a.m. She had never slept this late before, but sometimes, your body needed that time to rejuvenate. Gracie walked into the kitchen and knew she immediately needed a hot cup of tea and a warm piece of toast. She gathered everything on a small tray and headed to the living room to sit and prepare herself for the day.

Gracie heard a door slam and, then, heard the footsteps. As she took a bite of her toast, the sound of the steps grew closer. *Is it a neighbor? Is it Anna coming over to share the morning? Who could it be?*

The doorbell rang and Gracie's heart nearly jumped from her chest. She walked to the door, a little bit leery, and, then, peeked through the side window – it was Logan!

It's Logan. Oh my goodness, what am I going to do? He was going to see her, plain and disheveled from sleep. No, he couldn't. The doorbell rang again with a little bit more enthusiasm. Gracie knew she had to open the door. She swallowed her toast quickly and grabbed the handle of the door to open it. When she did, a small crumb got lodged, and Gracie began to cough a bit too much.

Logan immediately walked in, concern written on his face. "Gracie, are you okay? Do you need a drink of water or something?" Gracie was trying to compose herself and point to her cup of tea, all without success. Finally, Logan pushed past Gracie and found the kitchen. He opened the cabinet door where the glasses were and came back with a small glass of water. "Here, Gracie, drink this."

Gracie took a quick sip and looked at him, trying to reaffirm with her eyes she was going to be okay. *Holy smokes, one little crumb of toast sure can cause a lot of chaos.*

Gracie watched as Logan moved towards the front door to close it.

He turned around and came towards Gracie. Gracie began to walk backwards to the couch.

"I'm okay," she told Logan. "I swear, just a crumb went down the wrong way. I'm good." Logan was coming closer to her. Gracie knew she would have to sit down on the couch or fall backward on the couch.

Logan approached Gracie and gently took the drink out of her hand and laid the glass on top of the end table. He looked directly into Gracie's eyes. Gracie was going to fall. And it was not going to be on the couch. Gracie swayed forward a bit, and that was all Logan needed.

Logan's husky voice whispered, "I've been wanting to do this since the day I saw you enter the elevator."

"Do what?" Gracie thought, and, then, it happened. Logan kissed her with passion. His tongue immediately parted Gracie's full, tender lips and began ravishing them. Logan's hands caught Gracie's back as she leaned backwards from his pillage of her lips. With one swift move, Logan ran his hand tenderly underneath Gracie's shirt, and in one-millionth of a second, Gracie's silk bra had been unsnapped. Gracie took a deep breath. Logan's hand moved to feel the softness of Gracie's breast. He gently rubbed the tip of Gracie's nipple until it was full and taught with anticipation.

Gracie tilted her head back. Logan began to travel down the side of Gracie's neck and then to the center. The room was spinning, and Gracie could not stop it. The feeling of euphoria had taken control. Logan pulled Gracie tightly into his body. Gracie could feel Logan's desire. It was right there. Gracie thought, *So, this is what torment feels like.* She felt a warm, slow, growing desire and the anticipation of both bodies entwined as one.

Logan stopped, and Gracie looked at him. Had she done something wrong? Logan began to smile and said, "I've waited forever for this, Gracie, I can wait no longer." Gracie acknowledged his need with a small nod of her head. Logan looked at Gracie and said, "Show me your bedroom."

Gracie began to walk towards her bedroom. Logan followed. Upon entering her bedroom, Logan smiled to himself. The room was as he expected. It was colorful, decorated in pinks and purples, Gracie's favorite colors—he remembered from high school.

She had a bear in the middle of the bed. It was an old, vintage bear that had seen better days. As he drew closer to the bed, the bear brought back a fond memory. It was the bear Logan had given Gracie on her birthday. She had kept the bear. Gracie turned to look at Logan and saw his gaze focused on the bear. She never thought she would see Logan after high school, much less have Logan in her bedroom. The bear had been her only memory of Logan.

Logan looked at Gracie and said, "Come here". Gracie walked toward Logan. She knew what was about to happen. Should she tell Logan? Should she tell Logan she had not dated much since she left high school? Or for that matter, she didn't have time with college and her career? Logan saw Gracie thinking for a moment.

What is she thinking? Logan wondered. Logan walked to Gracie and placed both his hands on her waist.

"Gracie," he said, "you must know I want you. I need you. I need to feel you beneath me. I need to be inside the warmth of you. I need to feel what it's like to have you moan my name. You must know where this is going. I desire you. Can you not feel me? Let me touch you and show you."

Gracie nodded, and that's all Logan needed. His mouth covered Gracie's lips. His lips were everywhere. They were nibbling at her ear lobes. They were moving down the side of her neck. He asked Gracie to raise her arms, and she did so. Just like a small breath of air, Logan had slipped her shirt over her head. Gracie immediately placed her arms over her breasts.

"Don't," Logan said, "I want to see you." Gracie needed to tell Logan. She could not think of the words to tell him. Before she could, though, Logan gently pulled her arms from her breasts. "Perfect," he said.

Gracie felt as if the heat in her home had been turned on. She was very hot. Logan gently took his hand and moved his mouth to where his hand was - Logan's tongue captured Gracie's nipple. Logan began to suck and swirl with his tongue. Logan looked at Gracie's nipple. It was taut. It was hard, just like he was. Logan moved to the other side and performed the same sucking and swirling motion.

Gracie began to lean back, so Logan could have easier access to what he needed—and what Gracie most definitely needed. She could not stop herself. A small moan escaped Gracie. Logan began to untie Gracie's pajama bottoms. He slid her pants down, and while doing so, he began kissing Gracie's stomach. He kissed Gracie's bellybutton. He shimmied Gracie's pants to the ground and guided her to step out of them. He looked at Gracie's silk boyfriend panties. They were, of course, pink with polka dots.

Logan placed his hand inside Gracie's silk panties. He could feel how soft Gracie was. Gracie was saying something. Logan was not comprehending what Gracie was telling him. He was lost in what he was contemplating doing to Gracie's body. He placed his finger at the lip of Gracie's private entry. Logan heard Gracie's intake of breath. He began to make an in-and-out motion. Gracie's body betrayed her, and she moved with Logan's finger. Logan could tell when Gracie was moist. Logan had yet to enter Gracie with his finger, but he knew how she would feel. Just around his finger, she was tight. It was as if her body knew what was going to take place next.

Logan slid her panties down to her tiny ankles. Gracie stepped out, as he instructed her. Upon hearing Logan's request, Gracie became aware of what was taking place. Her body was betraying her. She felt an ache deep inside her. Gracie did not know what to say. She had never done anything like this. She had never experienced the emotions and feelings that she was experiencing at this very moment. When she looked at Logan, she could see the desire in his eyes. He looked as if he were going to devour her with those piercing eyes.

Logan began to take unbutton his shirt. It seemed like it was an eternity for his shirt to be removed. Gracie watched as Logan unbuttoned each button. Gracie knew what was under the shirt. She could already tell that Logan had a masculine physique. What else did the rest of Logan's body look like? Gracie's heart skipped a beat. She was about to find out. Logan took his shirt off, and Gracie was taken aback by the need she felt to touch Logan. Gracie did not move as she watched Logan undo his belt and, then, unzip his pants. Logan removed his pants and was just in his boxers. Gracie could not take her eyes off Logan. She looked at Logan and saw his desire for her. Logan was not small. Gracie was not sure why her eyes were immediately drawn to Logan's manhood.

Logan began to walk towards Gracie again, and in one swift motion, Logan embraced Gracie in one of the most passionate moments Gracie had ever experienced. Nothing, nor no one had prepared Gracie for all the emotions and feelings that were taking place. Logan reached around Gracie's waist and nudged her towards the bed. He placed his hand behind Gracie's waist and lowered her onto the bed. Gracie watched as Logan removed his boxers and placed protection over his manhood. Gracie did not have time to think why Logan would have protection on hand.

Logan began to pull Gracie in an upward motion to have better access to lay Gracie on the bed. Gracie could not pull her eyes away from Logan. She waited breathlessly for Logan to lower himself on her bed. Gracie knew the exact moment when Logan's body was going to touch hers. She felt his hands as he placed them on her bed to steady himself. Gracie instinctively knew Logan was going to kiss her, and he was not going to stop with just a kiss. Gracie thought to herself that she wanted a lot more than a kiss. Her body wanted more.

Logan smiled and looked at Gracie and lowered his head to taste those soft cherry lips. Logan knew Gracie would taste sweet—and not just on her lips. He began the kiss with intent and, then, the kiss grew more passionate. Logan nipped Gracie's lips with his and felt her intake of breath. His hand moved down the curve of Gracie's breast and gently placed the nipple between his thumb and forefinger. Gracie's nipple became swollen. Logan knew Gracie wanted him. She was moving her body in time with Logan's.

Logan moved his hand over Gracie's tummy. He moved his head down to kiss her belly button. Gracie could not believe this was happening. In high school, she had wondered what it would be like to kiss Logan, but this, this was beyond wonder, beyond her thoughts, beyond her dreams. Gracie did not know the direction Logan was taking with his kisses, but if this was heaven, she wanted to stay. Logan kissed the inside of Gracie's thighs and gently pushed her legs apart. Logan then moved back closer to the side of Gracie's neck.

Logan began a swirling motion right where Gracie's most sensual part was—right above the entry of her clitoris. He began slowly, at first. Gracie moaned. He took a step closer to insert his finger to feel her moistness. Using small and slow strokes in and out, Logan could feel Gracie's body respond. Gracie could not help the soft moan that escaped her lips.

"Please, Logan," she whispered. Logan looked deeply into Gracie's eyes.

"Please what, Gracie? Tell me what you want," Logan prompted her.

"I don't know," Gracie responded. "I need you." That was all that Logan needed to hear. Logan had waited a very long time to hear Gracie tell him she needed him.

Logan positioned himself to enter Gracie. Logan's need was evident. He was hard with desire for Gracie. As Logan entered Gracie, he felt it, and so did Gracie. Logan saw a small wince of pain from Gracie and, then, Logan knew.

Before Logan could go any further, he looked at Gracie with all the control he could muster in the heat of passion, "Gracie, are you a virgin?" Gracie was taken aback, because she was. She had never been intimate with anyone the way she was being with Logan. She had never had the desire to pursue a relationship, yet alone a sexual relationship. Gracie could not utter the word "yes". She nodded, waiting for Logan's reaction.

Logan smiled and kissed her nose. "Do you trust me?" Logan asked. Again, words escaped Gracie, and she nodded yes. "Listen to me, Gracie," Logan told her. "It will only hurt for a moment, but, then, the most unbelievable emotion will take over, and I will take your body to heights you never imagined."

Logan never took his eyes off Gracie as he entered her. A small whimper escaped Gracie, and Logan covered it with his kisses of reassurance and passion. Gracie could feel Logan inside of her. He was strong and sure of himself. Logan began moving in and out. The motion was slow, at first. Logan was giving Gracie time for her body to react to his hardness and begin the movements with him.

Gracie knew when Logan became more intent. His breathing changed. It was much more breathless. As Gracie felt the change, she knew something was about to happen that was going to change her life forever—especially her relationship with Logan. Gracie let Logan know she was ready to take him all.

She pulled Logan closer and whispered in his ear, "Now, please." With one thrust, Logan was there. That point of no return. The motions of Logan's hardness in and out sent Gracie over the edge. This frantic emotion for a sweet ending was mind-blowing.

Logan whispered to Gracie, "Look at me. I want to see you when I bring you to ecstasy." And with those last words, Logan plunged deep into Gracie's warmth and moistness. Gracie shivered. She now knew what Anna had meant when she told her there was no explanation for this feeling.

Logan rolled to Gracie's side and pulled her into him. It reminded Gracie of the word "spooning" that her grandmother had always talked about. She never understood what her grandmother meant, but as soon as she felt Logan's stomach against the small of her back, spooning would now be in her vocabulary. She felt Logan's hand slide along her waist and, then, cup her breast.

"Gracie, are you okay? Did I hurt you?" he asked.

Gracie turned towards Logan. "No, Logan," she replied, "you did not hurt me."

Logan kissed Gracie's shoulder, and Gracie knew he was going to ask. It was just hanging in the air. "Why didn't you tell me you were a virgin? I would have gone slower," Logan told her.

Gracie smiled and said, "You never asked me."

"Is there anything else you need to or want to tell me?" Logan chuckled.

"No, I think you know the most important thing," Gracie laughed.

As Gracie felt Logan intertwine his hand inside hers, she knew the moment Logan had relaxed enough to fall asleep. Gracie could not. Thoughts were crowding Gracie's mind. What would be the next step? What would happen in the morning when both had to get ready and arrive at work? So many issues racing in Gracie's mind. She finally fell asleep in the comfort and safety of Logan's body. Tomorrow would be a new day, and Gracie would handle it then.

When Gracie heard the alarm go off, she felt the weight of something across her stomach. Was she dreaming? She could not move. Then came the realization that not only was she nude, Logan's was nude, and both their bodies were wrapped tightly against each other.

Gracie went to hit the alarm for another ten-minute snooze, when she heard Logan say, "Good morning. Ready to start the day?" Shyly, Gracie nodded yes.

Logan threw back the covers and said, "Let's do this, then. Would you like to shower first, or would you like to shower with me?"

Gracie laughed and said, "I'm pretty sure I can shower without any help. If you need to shower first, Logan, that's fine."

Logan grinned and said, "Ladies first. I'll fix us breakfast. Chop, chop."

Gracie came out of the shower and was toweling off, when Logan opened the door and stated as a matter of fact, "My turn." Logan just dropped the towel he was wrapped in and proceeded to walk into the shower. Gracie's jaw dropped just as fast as Logan's towel. Logan looked directly at Gracie and repeated, "Are you sure you do not want to join me?"

Gracie thought about taking Logan up on his offer, but, then, they both would be late to the hospital. That would not be good. Gracie had never arrived late to work. Gracie told Logan, "It's okay. Finish your shower. I am going to get dressed and then, let's eat breakfast."

Logan nodded. Gracie went to her nightstand and pulled out her favorite silky pink panties and bra to wear. Pink was her favorite color, after all, and it felt like a pink day. As Gracie was finishing dressing, Logan stepped out of the shower and dressed.

Both walked to the kitchen, and, as Logan promised, there was breakfast. Bacon, biscuits, and fruit. Not bad. Simple and easy. Gracie and Logan finished breakfast and placed the dishes in the sink. Gracie brushed her teeth and moved to the side to allow Logan room to brush his teeth. As they were leaving Gracie's home, Logan walked toward his car and then turned around and walked back to open Gracie's car door.

Before Gracie knew it, Logan kissed her and said, "I'll see you at work. Don't be late." Logan made sure Gracie was in her car and, then, walked to his car and got in. He pulled out of Gracie's driveway, giving Gracie enough room to back out. Gracie began the trip to her haven. All the while, she could see Logan in her rearview mirror. For some unknown reason, it was comforting to know that Logan was behind her.

As Logan watched Gracie pull into the hospital parking lot, he was feeling something that was foreign to him. Logan was feeling a euphoria of happiness that he had not felt in a long time. He couldn't explain it—he just knew he was excited to be arriving at work with Gracie.

Logan waited for Gracie to walk inside the children's hospital ahead of him. For some reason, he felt Gracie needed time to assess all that had taken place. Logan knew he did. He watched the hospital doors open and Gracie walk through. He opened his car door and checked to be sure all was as it needed to be. As Logan walked through the doors of the children's hospital, his thoughts returned to the night and the wee hours of the morning. He knew Gracie had received pleasure. It was in the way she slept curled into his body. He could feel her breathing and, then, without knowing it, Gracie had curled her fingers into his.

Logan thought to himself that this would not be the last time he brought Gracie to moan his name. The fact that Gracie was a virgin made it more important to Logan to show Gracie what pleasure could truly feel like.

As Logan walked into the elevator, he shook his head. Lord, he needed to concentrate on his tasks and children, not Gracie. With that thought, Logan pushed the button for the third floor and wondered what the day would hold.

Goodness, what a morning, Gracie thought. It felt as if kids were falling from the heavens. From broken ankles and arms, to sprained wrists, to high fevers, to sniffly noses, the hospital was being hit from every which way. Gracie looked up at the clock. Her stomach had been telling her it was time to eat. Gracie told Anna she was headed to the cafeteria for a quick lunch.

As Logan was finishing paperwork on his last patient, a small child who had decided to swallow five pennies—because his brother had dared him—Logan felt the stabs of hunger. His stomach had been telling him it was time to eat. Logan told the nurse on call with him that he was headed to the cafeteria for a quick lunch.

Gracie walked to the elevator and pushed the first floor. All she could think about was that she was starvin' marvin. The doors closed, and Gracie's thoughts went back to morning. Watching Logan come out of the shower—her shower—with just a towel wrapped around his body, and the towel he had used did not cover all of Logan. It left just enough to the imagination as to what was under that towel. Gracie blushed to herself, because she knew. She knew exactly what was under that towel. Pleasure, pure pleasure.

Gracie's assignment had been the seventh floor today. The elevator seemed like it was taking forever. Six, five, four, three- the elevator stopped on the third floor. The doors opened, and Gracie looked to see who would be stepping on. It was Logan. There was no one else on the elevator. It was just going to be her and Logan. They were going to be alone.

This was not good. Gracie had not had enough time to ponder the evening's events—or for that matter, the morning's events—adequately. The elevator felt very small and confining. Logan didn't look up until he took a step onto the elevator. When he did, his dark blue eyes pierced Gracie's entire being. She was frozen. Her legs would not move. What was happening? Logan smiled what Gracie felt was a very devilish smile. She looked at him, and the next words from Logan melted Gracie.

"I see you're hungry, too," Logan commented. "I'm hungry, but not for food." It took a moment for Gracie to realize what his words meant, and, then, it dawned on her. Logan was not talking about food, like a hamburger or grilled cheese. Logan was talking about her.

Gracie looked at Logan and wanted to let him know that what happened between them should not happen again. After all, they both worked at the same hospital. Gracie knew rumors would spread, and she did not want that. Rumors were gossip, and Gracie hated gossip.

Gracie started to say something, but Logan walked towards her with determination. Without even looking, the doors closed, and Logan pushed the button to hold the elevators. At that point, it hit Gracie. She was alone with Logan on an elevator with very little room. Should she panic now or later?

Logan looked at Gracie and said, "You cannot go anywhere, Gracie. Come here".

Gracie looked at Logan. It was just two little bitty steps, and she would be face-to-face with Logan. Again, she could not move. Logan must have read her mind and her indecision, because before Gracie knew it, Logan had pulled her into his chest.

"You smell like the morning, Gracie," he whispered in her ear. Gracie slightly turned her face into Logan's lips, where the whisper had come from. Logan took this small gesture as an okay to nibble on the lobe of Gracie's ear. The small intake of her breath had confirmed what Logan knew—that Gracie desired him.

Logan pushed Gracie to the back of the elevator wall. Gracie could not balance herself. She placed both her hands on the metal rail to keep herself from falling forward into Logan. Logan placed both his hands on the wall of elevator. Gracie saw the look in Logan's eyes. He was going to kiss her. Gracie closed her eyes. She inhaled Logan's scent. He had showered in her body wash that morning. The kiss was slow and tender at first.

Gracie knew when it changed. Logan grabbed her waist and pulled her into him. "I've thought about you all morning, Gracie, have you thought about me?"

Gracie shook her head sideways, meaning "no", but she was lying. She had not stopped thinking about Logan. He was everywhere in her mind and thoughts. Logan took his thumb and rubbed it over Gracie's bottom lip.

"You're lying, Gracie. Tell me you thought about me." Gracie was too shy to admit it to him. Gracie knew she did not have a lot of knowledge in the dating arena, but she didn't want Logan to know how much, in this particular setting, she wanted him. Logan smiled and laughed a warm, soft chuckle. "You feel it. You feel me. You know I want you," Logan spoke.

Gracie realized they were in a public elevator—the hospital's elevator— and at some point, those doors were going to open. "Logan," Gracie said his name, "we cannot. The elevator. The doors are going to open."

Logan stopped what he was doing and looked at Gracie. "Worried about your reputation, are you? What would your friends say, what would the staff think– is that what you are worried about, because it is the furthest thing from my mind at this moment," he stated.

Gracie did not want to let him know that she was almost to the edge of just telling Logan to take her in the elevator. The intake of her breath, when Logan's hand cupped her left buttock, gave Logan all the confirmation he needed. Logan pulled her slowly into him, with intent, so she could feel Logan's need. Gracie didn't know why, but she lifted her leg, so Logan could entwine his body into hers. Logan's left hand was holding Gracie steadily against him.

Logan needed to taste Gracie. He thrust his tongue in to Gracie's open, inviting mouth. He swirled his tongue around Gracie's, waiting for her response. An intake of her breath, and Gracie responded with all her being. The kiss was as heated and as filled with passion as if it were a "last kiss goodbye". Logan's hand shot under Gracie's scrubs, up her breast. The alarm went off on the elevator. The elevator had been holding too long.

Immediately, Gracie pulled away and looked at Logan. "What are we doing?" she asked.

Logan laughed a throaty laugh and responded, "You don't know?" He pushed the button to take the elevator off of hold. Logan looked at Gracie and said, "You may want to…" Before Logan could finish the sentence, the doors of the elevator opened.

Standing on the other side was Anna. Logan had positioned himself back against the rails. Gracie was in the corner. Anna walked in and smiled and looked at Gracie. Gracie looked a bit disheveled. Was she not feeling good? Anna leaned into Gracie and whispered, "Everything okay?"

Gracie could not audibly answer. She just nodded her head "yes". Gracie could not believe what had just happened. She had just allowed Logan to do the almost unspeakable to her in her work elevator. Sex—pure, unadulterated sex—in an elevator. Gracie looked over at Logan, who had a devilish smile on his face.

"Right now, I want to throttle you," Gracie whispered underneath her breath, so only Logan could hear her.

Logan winked at Gracie and mouthed the words, "Wait 'til next time."

Gracie shook her head vehemently "no". There was not going to be a next time. Not at her home, and definitely not in the elevator. Not ever again as far as Gracie was concerned. Logan seemed just a little bit too smug in thinking that Gracie would fall into his arms on a whim. That was not going to happen. If Logan thought she was just going to swoon over him, he was mistaken.

Gracie looked at Anna and said, "Are you hungry?"

Anna said, "Well, of course. It's lunch time—isn't that why you're on the elevator?"

Gracie looked at Logan and, then, at Anna and replied, "Absolutely, why else would I be on the elevator?"

Logan turned to Gracie and Anna and stated, "I could think of other things." His answer was directed at Gracie.

Anna looked at Gracie and asked, "Did I miss something?"

"No, you didn't' Anna, let's get some lunch," Gracie replied.

As soon as the doors opened, Gracie almost ran through them. She started to stumble, but Logan caught her on the tip of her elbow. "I got you," Logan told her.

Just that one touch, his touch – *Good lawd, Gracie, get a grip on yourself,* she thought.

She looked at Anna and said, "Let's go."

Gracie did not look back to see if Logan had stepped off the elevator yet or not. She needed not to have Logan close to her while eating. Gracie needed some girl time. She wanted to hear how Anna's day had been.

Gracie and Anna went through the cafeteria line. Gracie only ordered a sandwich, chips, and water. Anna, on the other hand, ordered a hamburger, French fries, and a chocolate milkshake. They found two empty spots to sit down. Gracie made sure it was only two empty spots. There was no way Logan could have lunch with them.

As Gracie and Anna began to talk about the day and what the rest of the week held and possible plans for the weekend, Gracie couldn't help but seek Logan out to see where he had landed. As Anna was discussing what they could do over the weekend, Gracie quickly perused the cafeteria in search of Logan. Gracie could not find him. When Gracie and Anna had exited the elevator, Gracie was sure that Logan had stepped out and was behind them. The more Anna talked, the more Gracie sought Logan's whereabouts.

Finally, Anna waved her hand in front of Gracie's face. "He's not here. He walked to the parking lot."

"Who?" Gracie asked Anna.

"Seriously, Gracie, you are going to ask me 'who'? You haven't heard one word I've said. You have been searching the cafeteria looking for him this entire time.

Gracie looked at Anna and asked, "Is it obvious?" Gracie knew she had not given full attention to Anna's conversation. She apologized. Anna was the only one who knew when something was not right with Gracie. Gracie was forever grateful for the friendship they shared.

Anna, said "It's okay. I understand there is something special taking place."

"I'm sorry. Let's finish eating and finalize our weekend plans, Gracie responded. As they finished lunch and made plans to attend a concert, Gracie could not help but wonder where Logan disappeared to.

As Gracie and Anna were gathering their trays, from the corner of her eye, Gracie saw Logan walking towards the main entrance of the children's hospital. Logan was not alone. He was walking and speaking with one of the Directors of Nursing (DNs, as they liked to be called). Gracie could not tell which one, but from the way Logan was laughing, there must have been something quite funny they were speaking about.

Without warning, Gracie experienced something she had never felt. Jealousy. She did not like Logan getting chummy with the DON. *What is going on with me?* Gracie thought. This was an emotion that Gracie never allowed. She had never felt jealous of any of her friends' relationships with their boyfriends. She had never felt jealousy about a promotion of a friend in the hospital. Gracie was always excited for them. This was foreign to Gracie. For whatever reason, Gracie could not take her eyes off Logan in the parking lot.

Anna nudged Gracie in the side. "Are you ready? If you keep staring, he's going to know you're watching him."

Gracie could not deny Anna's statement. She looked at Anna and said, "Yes, let's go, before I do something I'll regret."

Anna chuckled to herself. "Good idea," she stated. "Don't want him to think you're worried about him or something."

Gracie rolled her eyes and said, "Right, whatever. Let's get back to our shift."

Logan did not go directly to the cafeteria. He had walked outside to get a breath of fresh air. Much more time in that elevator with Gracie and all of the world would have seen way too much of both of them. As he was walking to the car to get his change of clothes for the gym, the Director of Nursing approached him and told Logan she had received his confirmation of his next assignment. Logan had not realized that he would know this soon where he would next be travelling.

As a travelling nurse, Logan had experienced visiting many amazing cities and some of the most renowned children's hospitals. Every transfer was a learning experience. Every child he met played an important part as to why Logan chose the life of a travel nurse. The children and their tenacity to bounce back from the illness or disease always brought Logan an appreciation of compassion. Most of the children would leave and go home and begin all over again with their next adventure. But there were always one or two who did not leave. They remained in the hospital. The hospital would become their home. The hospital would become the place where their mom and dad would take turns showering and running home to bring in extra items, realizing they were in for the long haul. Clothes, snacks, video games, movies, and a favorite blankie or stuffed animal were always the go-to items.

Logan remembered a beautiful little girl who had been brought in for a broken leg. When they had completed the x-rays, they found cancer in her small, tiny leg. She was only five years old. Logan knew what the outcome would be. Aggressive chemo began, but the cancer spread quickly. She never left the hospital. It was times like this that Logan knew what his purpose was. Upon realizing she would never leave the hospital, Logan and the rest of the staff made sure she was kept busy with painting, coloring, and watching her favorite movies. Afterwards, the family had sent a basket to the hospital, along with a card thanking the staff for their kindness toward their daughter.

Logan shook his head just a bid. The past was the past. The present was in front of him. Full of new adventures and growth for his career. But this day, Logan did not feel that usual excitement of packing everything up and travelling to another city. He really liked Pioneer Children's Hospital. He loved the staff. He did not know exactly why, but leaving this hospital was going to be different than the others. Just like with all assignments as a travelling nurse, Logan knew it would be about four to six more weeks before the actual transfer from Denver to the next hospital would occur. According to the paperwork, the next hospital would be Blessings Hospital in New York City. This was a children's hospital that Logan had submitted to twice and had never been placed in the rotation. The hospital was known for its heart and lung transplants performed on children. Today, though, it was confirmed: he would be going to a dream job and dream hospital.

Logan walked back into Pioneer Children's Hospital. He stepped on the elevator and pushed the fifth floor. Logan had been working on both the fourth and fifth floors. The only time he had seen Gracie today was on the elevator. Logan grabbed his clipboard, and off he went to begin checking in on the children. He had to be sure they had eaten their lunch. Sometimes, if they did not like what was being served, the children would try hiding their food in their napkin. Logan smiled, because the children thought he would not catch on to that idea. Little did they know, he had tried that with his mom when he did not like something he was trying for the first time.

As the day wore on and paperwork was complete and last-minute rounds finished, Logan's thoughts wandered to what Gracie would be doing tonight. Logan looked at the staff and said good night. He grabbed his gym back and started towards the elevators. He pushed the button, and when the doors opened, he automatically walked in and pushed the button for the first floor. Logan was so lost in his thoughts he did not realize the elevator had not stopped on the first floor, but had stopped on the second floor. This was where ICU was located. The doors opened, and there she was.

Logan smiled at her and said, "Come on in."

Gracie smiled hesitantly and scanned the elevator. There was no one else in this elevator. Again, it was just her and Logan. Gracie walked on and immediately stood towards the front of the doors of the elevator. She did not need to be close to Logan, and she definitely needed an escape route. Logan chuckled as he saw what she did. He decided not to grab her and kiss her passionately, which was what he wanted to do. He had missed Gracie. He hated to admit that to himself. Logan enjoyed seeing her. Logan enjoyed talking "shop" with Gracie. Gracie was very intelligent, but more than that, she was kind and compassionate.

Logan decided to try a different approach to get Gracie's attention. "Are you hungry, Gracie? We could go grab a quick bite."

Gracie was hungry. But not for what Logan was asking. She had missed seeing Logan today. She was concerned about what had taken place during lunch today with Logan and the DON. She turned to look at Logan. That was a mistake. Gracie was lost in those deep blue eyes as soon as she began to say no.

She stopped and nodded, "I could use a quick fix. I am a bit hungry."

"Well, okay then, let's go. I know a great little mom-and-pop restaurant not too far from where you live," Logan told her. He then asked Gracie if she would just like to ride with him, instead of both of them driving their cars.

Gracie said, "Sure, I'm tired, and it will be nice to rest on the way."

As they walked towards Logan's car, he placed the small of his hand on her back to guide her towards the passenger side. He opened the door for her, waited for her to get in, and, then, closed the door for her. *Really*, Gracie thought, *he's a gentleman, too. I'm doomed.* Gracie was such a sucker for the old-school type. A guy who opened and closed the doors for a woman, whether it be on a vehicle or entering a business or a restaurant – it was just plain nice. Gracie took a deep breath and closed her eyes. At last, a brief moment of relaxation.

She heard the door open and looked as Logan sat down. Without thought, Logan reached across Gracie's body. Gracie inhaled. *What is he doing?*

Logan laughed. "Don't worry, I'm not going to do anything Gracie. I just want to fasten your seatbelt before we take off. You forgot." Gracie looked at him as his arm came across her bosom and he snapped the seatbelt in. Her intake of breath was a sign that Logan wanted to hear in a more intimate spot, not in the car. Logan looked at Gracie. "All good. We are set to go. You ready?" Gracie nodded. She didn't know if she was ready or not.

As Logan approached Poppy's Restaurant, Gracie looked at the country outside of the restaurant. How had she missed this little mom-and-pop dive? Logan parked and immediately got out and told Gracie he would get the door. Okay, now this was too much. Logan was not real. He could not be. That's twice. As Gracie stepped out of the car, she lost her balance just a bit and fell into Logan's chest.

"Steady," he said. "The night is just beginning." Gracie placed her hands on his chest to push away.

"I'm okay. I just misplaced my footing."

Logan looked at her and held her hands against his chest. "I'll always catch you, Gracie," he promised. As they approached the entrance of Poppy's, Logan grabbed the door and said, "After you, my lady." Three times he had shown how kind he was.

This is a dream, Gracie thought to herself. *Sooner or later the true "man" will reveal himself.* Logan and Gracie entered and received a warm welcome from the owner, Poppy, himself.

"Where would you like to sit?" Poppy asked them. "Booth or table?"

"Booth, please," Logan stated. Gracie slide into the booth Poppy assigned them. She fully expected Logan to sit on the other side, but that was not in the case. Logan slid right in beside Gracie. As he was sliding in, Gracie knew his body would be right next to hers. She was right: his right leg was touching her left leg. This was going to be torture. Was she going to be able to eat?

Logan slid into the booth beside Gracie on purpose. He wanted to feel her next to him. He wanted to be beside Gracie. He wanted to be inside of Gracie. He wanted to feel Gracie's warmth surround his entire being. Logan was feeling all kinds of ways and could not place his finger on any one thing other than that he needed to eat fast and he needed Gracie's touch.

Logan and Gracie ordered their food. Just a sandwich and chips and drink – something simple and fast. The food came. Logan watched as Gracie took a bite of her sandwich. Oh yes, Gracie could bite him. She could bite his lips. She could nibble on his ears. Gracie could just nibble wherever she desired. Logan smiled a bit to himself. Gracie noticed.

"What are you smiling about, Logan?" she asked him. Logan looked at her as if he were going to devour her, Gracie thought.

He replied, "If I told you, you would blush from head to toe." Gracie already knew what Logan was thinking. She was thinking the same thing. She really needed to get out of the booth. She was slowly sinking into Logan's eyes and could feel the heat from his leg touching hers intimately. His leg was not pressing up against her, but was ever so lightly brushing against her. Gracie took another bite, and that was it. It was all Logan could handle. "Gracie, if we do not leave here now, I am going to take you in front of God and everyone here in Poppy's."

Gracie looked at Logan. No words formed on her lips. What was she to say to that? She was thinking the same thing. If Logan did not take her now, Gracie was going to fall off the edge of the booth. All she could do was nod in agreement. That was all Logan needed to place cash on the table with a huge tip.

"Thank you, Poppy. It was great. Sorry to rush out." Poppy smiled. Poppy knew what was going on. He knew that feeling of "first love". It was written all over the young lady's face. On Logan's face was the desire of a man for a woman. Poppy wished them good night and turned around to finish his task at hand.

As they were walking towards Logan's car, Logan stopped Gracie in the middle of the parking lot. He said, "Tell me to come home with you, Gracie. Tell me you want me. Tell me you desire to feel me inside of you. Tell me, Gracie."

Gracie had never had a man talk to her as though she were his last reason for living. This could not be happening. Gracie looked at Logan. "You know I do."

"Say it," Logan told her. "Say it looking at me."

Gracie looked at Logan with all the intensity and desire she had and said the words Logan had longed to hear from her sweet lips, "Yes, Logan, I want you."

Logan looked at Gracie and said, "Let's go home."

The drive to Gracie's home seemed to take forever. It was less than five miles from Poppy's to Gracie's. It felt like eternity. Logan pulled into Gracie's driveway and turned the car off. He looked over at Gracie. Desire was written in Logan's look. Gracie waited for Logan to open her door. She knew he would. This small gesture was one of the largest gestures in Gracie's book. It made an impression on her. Logan was a gentleman. Gracie stepped out of Logan's car, and Logan closed the door and placed his hand on the small of Gracie's back and guided her to the front door. Gracie fumbled for the keys in her purse. Logan placed his hand on hers.

"Gracie, look at me," he said. "Let me find the keys. Let's go inside and just relax."

Gracie nodded. She did not know why she was so jumpy. What was she expecting? For Logan to ravish her tonight is the thought that came to Gracie's mind.

Logan opened the front door. "After you," he said. Gracie turned on the light to the living room and headed to the kitchen to get a bottle of water. Working in the health industry, Gracie tried to stay away from caffeine and soft drinks. She did try to eat healthy. Some days that she worked in the children's hospital turned into nights as well, especially when there were so many sick children at once. Her body needed to be prepared for these weird shift hours.

As she entered the living room, Logan had already made himself comfortable on her couch. Logan looked at Gracie and patted the cushion. "Have a seat, I won't bite," he said.

Gracie smiled, "I know you won't. I just need to get my blanket and change into something comfy." Logan watched as Gracie disappeared into her bedroom. Within less than two minutes—which Logan thought was a pretty fast change—Gracie emerged in her matching hot pink and black polka-dotted sweatpants and henley tee. Logan didn't think Gracie could look any sexier than in that moment.

Gracie looked at Logan. She knew he was thinking something, but she did not want to ask what. Gracie walked towards Logan and sat at the opposite end of the couch. Logan had the remote control and had turned the television on to a movie that was just getting ready to begin. Gracie looked at Logan and asked what the movie was about. She really didn't care what the movie was about. It was just small talk. Logan told her it was an action chick flick.

Gracie shook her head and said, "It seems like a great combination. Action and chick flick." Gracie asked Logan if he would like a water as well. She apologized that she did not have anything stronger, nor anything with caffeine. Logan was impressed. He told Gracie he was fine.

The movie began, and Logan reached for Gracie's hands. "Come here,

Gracie. Nothing's going to happen, I promise." Gracie scooted closer to Logan. They both were right in the middle of her couch. Logan touched Gracie's face and kissed the tip of her nose. "I promise nothing will happen, unless you want it," Logan told her.

Gracie trusted Logan. She knew he was a man of his word. He had never betrayed her in high school. Gracie knew Logan was honest. As the movie began, Gracie caught her herself nodding off a bit, until finally she could not stop from leaning into Logan's broad, strong shoulders. Logan did not want to move. If he moved, he would wake Gracie. He did not want to disturb her beautiful slumber. Gracie's breathing was soft against his shoulder.

She turned to snuggle into Logan, and he gently led her head to be placed in his lap. He realized his lap may not be the best place to lay Gracie's head. He hoped Gracie did not feel how much he wanted her. This would definitely wake her up, Logan smiled to himself. The movie finished. Logan turned the television off. He did not want anything to disturb Gracie, nor the serene look of peace on her face.

Gracie was beautiful, Logan thought to himself. Her eyes were the bluest of the blues. They held the color of the sky on an early spring morning. Gracie's nose was perfect. Her lips were full and soft. A perfect little indentation that formed a small heart. Logan took a small piece of Gracie's hair that had covered her face and pulled it to the side. Gracie turned her face into the palm of Logan's hand. Logan thought to himself all the things he had wanted to do to Gracie tonight, but when he looked at her sleeping so peacefully, he knew this was not the time. There would be another time, he was sure of it. Logan had wanted a restful night with no interruptions. Logan had wanted to talk to Gracie about what had happened with the DON today.

Logan knew he needed to get Gracie into her own bed. He gently shifted his body, in order to pull Gracie in an upward position to be enveloped against his chest. He then placed one arm underneath her legs and positioned himself to rise with Gracie.

As he lifted her and began to walk towards Gracie's bedroom, Gracie placed her hand against Logan's chest, "Please don't leave. Please stay," she said.

Logan did not know if he had heard Gracie correctly or not. As he lay Gracie down on her bed, he pulled the covers back and tugged her legs under the covers. She immediately rolled onto her side. Logan checked everything to be sure all was well before he left. But then, he heard Gracie say, "Please don't leave. Please stay."

Logan smiled. He wanted to stay. He wanted to protect Gracie. Logan took off his shirt and jeans. Typically, Logan slept in the nude, but he thought it may scare Gracie, should she awake and not realize how she had gotten into her bed, nor how Logan had gotten there. The boxers would be fine. Logan drew the covers back and laid down.

As soon as Logan's body came in contact with Gracie's, Gracie turned and spooned her body into Logan's. Her breathing was soft and quiet. "Safe" was the first word that came to Logan's mind. Gracie was safe, next to him. Logan laid his hand over Gracie's abdomen and pulled her closer to him. She did not reject Logan pulling her closer. Logan did not know the time, he only knew he was at the right place at the right time. He was with Gracie. With that thought, Logan dozed off to sleep.

Gracie went to turn her body, but something was blocking her movement. Was it one of the pillows that had gotten caught in between the covers? Gracie continued to move around, trying to shift her body into a more relaxed state, and, then, she knew it was not a pillow. It was Logan. Logan was cupping her right breast. And his hand was not still.

Logan was swirling his thumb around the tip of Gracie's nipple. Her nipple was responding on its own. Gracie did not know if Logan was awake or not, but she was. Her entire body was awake. Logan's thumb left Gracie's nipple and his hand travelled to Gracie's belly button. His thumb explored her belly button, just like it had explored her breast and nipple. He made small, circular motions, and, then, his fingers hit the edge of Gracie's panties.

She inhaled deeply, and Logan knew Gracie was awake. Gracie knew Logan was awake, too. His manhood was pressing into Gracie. Gracie knew what that feeling was. Logan's fingers gently pulled the edge of her panties up from her skin, so he would have easier access to her privates. Logan felt the brush of Gracie's pubic hairs and knew where heaven would lie. Logan gently began a sliding motion on the outer lip of Gracie's clitoris.

Logan felt Gracie's position change, and her awareness of what was taking place. Without realizing what she was doing, Gracie's body started moving in unison with the path of Logan's finger. Up and down in gentle, slow motions. Logan knew that this was just the beginning of what he wanted Gracie to feel on this Saturday morning. He did not want to stop, but he felt that Gracie should be aware of how her body was betraying her, and she needed to be awake.

Logan whispered in the back of her ear, "Are you awake, Gracie?" Without turning around, Gracie nodded her head. Logan knew she would probably not look at him, because her body was doing most of the talking. Logan gently touched Gracie's shoulder. "Gracie, turn around," Logan implored. Gracie knew as soon as she did, her body and the blush of her cheeks would betray her. Gracie rolled over and looked intently into Logan's baby blue eyes. Gracie could get lost in Logan's eyes like a kid at Disney World.

Logan took the tip of his thumb and rubbed it across Gracie's bottom lip.

Her lips were full and swollen. Logan knew Gracie's lips were waiting for him. He was going to devour those luscious lips—and not just the ones on her pretty face. As Logan drew near to Gracie, he took his hand and slowly separated her legs. He looked at Gracie and positioned himself over her. He was balancing his weight and his desire at the same time. As the tip of Logan entered Gracie, Gracie inhaled her breath.

"I need to feel you inside of me, Logan, please," Gracie begged Logan.

Logan needed to feel all of Gracie's warmth wrapped around him. It was as if time stood still. Logan thrust one time and felt Gracie's body shift to accommodate his size. When she felt all of him inside of her, Gracie knew that was no other feeling like this. Logan began moving in and out, slowly at first, and, then, it became a game as to who could please who first. Gracie's arms were wrapped around Logan's back. She was, without realizing it, creating the climax for Logan. Gracie had wrapped her legs around Logan. When she did, Logan had access to the sweetest spot. He could feel Gracie match his thrusts. He could feel Gracie become moist. Logan had been holding back, but he could no longer. In one plunge into heaven, Logan climaxed. Gracie knew when sweetness had entered her entire being.

As they lay entwined in each other's arms, Gracie asked Logan, "May I ask you a question about the other day when you were outside in the parking lot with the DON?"

What an unusual question to ask me about, Logan thought. He responded, "Sure, what would you like to know?" Gracie was having second thoughts about asking, but she knew if she didn't, she would be curious.

"Logan, what were you talking about?" Logan knew he had been putting off the inevitable. He did not want to discuss what he knew Gracie probably knew already.

Logan looked at Gracie and said, "We were discussing my next travel assignment."

Gracie's heart sank. She knew that Logan was a travelling nurse. She had heard about these positions, but she had decided early on in her career that this type of nursing career was not for her. Gracie loved coming into work at the children's hospital. She loved all the friends she had made. More importantly, Gracie had become attached to several of the children while they were there. Gracie knew their likes, favorite foods, favorite movies, favorite heroes. Gracie needed that consistency. She had been approached about becoming a travel nurse, but Gracie knew home is where the heart lies. It sounded corny, but that's who Gracie was.

Logan told Gracie, "I'm sorry I didn't tell you." Gracie was upset that Logan had not confided in her. As soon as he had said, "next travel assignment", he saw Gracie's persona deflate. It was not like Logan had kept it a secret from Gracie. Gracie knew this was a temporary assignment. And then it happened: Gracie got out of bed, without even looking at Logan. She walked to the shower and turned the water on. She then shut the bathroom door. Logan had thought this was going to be a great morning. Based on how these last few minutes had played out, it was *not*.

Logan heard the shower stop and heard Gracie rummaging around in the bathroom. He could hear her talking to herself. This definitely was not good. As he heard the door open, he looked directly at Gracie, who, at this point, was already dressed in her sweatpants and shirt and, just in that short timeframe, had put her sneakers on. Logan stared at Gracie in disbelief. She was quick dresser.

Gracie looked at Logan. "I'm going for a run," she told him. "I don't know when I'll be back. As for my car and retrieving it from the hospital parking lot, I'll get Anna to take me. Don't worry about me. Be sure to let yourself out. Feel free to take a shower, if you need."

Before Logan could even utter one word, Gracie had walked through the hallway and out the front door. He heard the click of the door. There was going to be hell to pay. Logan just knew it. He could tell by the way Gracie was gritting her teeth, without realizing it, and the way she had looked at him.

Logan got up. He decided to take Gracie up on her offer to shower and, then, he would leave. As he was shaving and rinsing the hair out of the sink (goodness forbid he did something else to upset Gracie), he knew they were going to have to address their relationship. Logan smiled. Was it a relationship? Yes, for all intents and his purpose, it was a relationship. Logan dressed and made sure everything was as it had been the night before. Clean, neat, tidy, and all in place and order – just like Gracie was. He double checked the bathroom to be sure. There was no way Gracie was going to complain about him leaving something that did not belong or was out-of-place. Logan made sure the front door was locked. He opened his car door, and as he was about to get in, he saw Gracie down the street, headed towards her home.

As she approached his car, she was out of breath from running, but she had enough energy to say, "Don't, don't you even dare try. I don't want to talk about last night, and I don't want to talk about your conversation with the DON."

Logan watched as Gracie walked up the sidewalk to the steps to her front porch. She did have such a cute walk and a cute butt to go along with that determined walk. Logan made sure Gracie got inside. He heard the lock click, which meant he was not going back up those steps. What in the world was he going to do with Gracie?

The weekend had passed in a flurry. Gracie had needed to call Anna to come pick her up, so she could drive to the hospital parking lot to retrieve her car. Anna kept giving sideways glances to Gracie. Gracie knew Anna wanted to ask questions. Gracie also knew Anna wanted answers. She just did not feel like discussing. Anna had picked upon that. Gracie was grateful that Anna knew not to ask. Anna sensed this was not a good time to be discussing the car and why she was driving Gracie back to the hospital on a weekend to pick up her car. Anna knew it had to be about Logan. Anna knew. Gracie was in love. Gracie was in love with Logan. She just couldn't admit it to herself.

Before she knew it, Gracie heard the alarm go off on Monday morning. *Not yet*, she thought to herself. *Just a few more minutes.* She pushed the snooze button two more times and, then, thought to herself, *I have to do this. I'm going to work, knowing that he is going to be leaving. I don't have to see him. I do have to work though.* Within less than 20 minutes, she was out the door and driving to the children's hospital. It was going to be a cool day.

As Logan pulled into the hospital parking lot, he caught himself searching for Gracie's car. He did not see it. Gracie usually arrived before him. This was not the case today. Logan wondered if everything from the weekend had had an effect on Gracie. Over the weekend, he could do nothing but think of Friday evening and all that had transpired. He could do nothing but think of Gracie and the sweetness he had tasted.

Logan shook his head. Time to start the day. He walked in through the hospital doors and knew it was going to be a "Monday". It seemed as though everyone was moving rather fast and with intent. He walked towards the elevator and pushed the third floor. He only had one more week here at Pioneer Children's Hospital. He would be leaving.

Gracie pulled into the hospital parking lot. She was running ten minutes behind. This was not like her. She was always early. But for some reason this morning, she just did not want to get to work as early as she had been doing. Gracie knew why. She did not want to see him or run into him. As she approached the parking spot, Gracie parked and turned the car off. It was instinct, but something was going to happen today. Gracie had an uneasy feeling. She sat for a moment, thinking, *Maybe if I don't go in and sit in the car all day, then nothing bad can happen.* Well, that wasn't going to happen. She gathered her belongings, opened the door and began the walk to the entry of the hospital doors.

Gracie got on the elevators. She pushed the button for the third floor, where she had always been assigned. As she stepped off the floor, Gracie knew something was not right. She immediately saw Anna, who had a worried look on her face. Anna approached Gracie and told her to put her things away. She needed in her Room 310. Room 310 was where a young boy had been admitted last Friday night for a football injury. The young boy had been hit head-on. According to his coach and family, after the hit, he did not move. He had remained unconscious in the ambulance. Upon arrival, he had been admitted and put on life support. The machine was breathing for him. Plain and simple in medical terms. There had been no change in brain activity. Gracie knew the outlook was not good, and now to see Anna's look of desperation – Gracie knew. The young boy was not going to make it.

Anna briefed Gracie on what had happened within just a span of two hours. The family had been called in. The doctor would be speaking with them about his chance of any type of recovery, if he would ever recover. Gracie never liked this part of her job. As she was listening to Anna, both Anna and Gracie knew when the family had arrived. The cries of the mother coming off the elevator were the signs that she knew what was about to take place. The mother approached the nurse's station and asked if they could see her son. Anna nodded "yes".

Anna grabbed Gracie's hand and said, "Please come with me." Anna and Gracie began the walk with the family to the little boy's room. The doctor was already in the room, checking the vitals and all the equipment that was keeping the young boy alive. Gracie pulled a chair, so the mom could be right beside her son. Anna motioned for the family to gather around. The doctor began the "talk". This was the talk of practical medicine. This was the informative talk. This was the talk that was so cold, as Gracie liked to refer to it. But then, she knew this doctor, and she knew he would then turn into a father, a father who was about to lose his son, a father who had dreamed of his son becoming the "all-star" football player. The dream had come to a halt. This was the mother's only son. This was the son who held her heart. This was all her love laying so peacefully in the bed.

The doctor looked at the family and told them what no family wants to hear, "I'm so sorry. There is no hope that he will recover. There is no brain activity. The machine is breathing for him. He is resting. We will leave you all to speak with him and hold him and let me know how we need to proceed on the young man's behalf."

Gracie knew the family needed this time to come to grips with what was about to happen. Gracie and Anna went back to their station and waited for the doctor. He looked at both Gracie and Anna. He thanked them for their compassion. Gracie and Anna had only met Dr. Nicholas Chrystmas this year, but his name was one you could not forget. Gracie always said he was one of the good guys. As Gracie heard the mom crying, she knew it was time. Dr. Chrystmas looked at both of them and began the walk. As they entered the room, Gracie knew the decision had been made to allow the young boy to pass.

Gracie was a Christian. She believed in God. She believed there was a heaven. Gracie quietly closed her eyes and asked the Lord to welcome the young boy with open arms. As Dr. Chrystmas turned the machine off, Gracie watched as the mom gently lay a kiss on her son's forehead and held his hand. This was so unfair. This would always be the part Gracie did not like, nor understand. Anna touched Gracie's hand, the small gesture that it was time to leave. Dr. Chrystmas would remain with the family.

As Gracie walked out of the young boy's room, she needed air. She felt the hospital walls closing in on her. She was going to suffocate if she did not get outside to smell the fresh air. Gracie told Anna she needed to take a quick break. Anna knew. Gracie always did this when there was a patient who was beyond hope. She nodded. Gracie grabbed her coat and belongings. She hit the down button with a bit too much enthusiasm, but it was not coming quick enough. The door opened and without looking, she pushed the button for the first floor. Gracie felt she was going to burst into tears. She did not want anyone to see her. Gracie did not know why she was so emotional.

Before the elevator doors could open, she heard his voice behind her. "Gracie, what's wrong? Gracie, tell me what's going on. Are you okay?" Logan was asking all sorts of questions.

Gracie had not even realized Logan was on the elevator when she stepped on. She had not raised her head to look to see who was on the elevator, if anyone. She mumbled under her breath, "I'm okay. Just need to take a quick break and get some fresh air."

Logan touched the tip of Gracie's elbow and turned her body towards his. He pushed a wayward piece of hair that had escaped Gracie's bun. "Tell me, Gracie. What can I do?"

Gracie just shook her head. She did not want to look at him. She had just lost a patient, and Logan would be leaving soon as well. Gracie knew this Monday was going to be unusual. So far, it was living up to the name "Manic Monday".

"Gracie, you are not leaving this elevator until you tell me what is going on," Logan implored.

That was it. That was all it took. Gracie looked at Logan with such sadness and emptiness. This was not his Gracie. Gracie was always smiling. She spoke to everyone, even if she didn't like them. He took Gracie's chin and tipped it up. Gracie looked at Logan with all the strength she could muster.

"I'm tired, Logan. I'm empty. I have nothing else to give. I have nothing to give you." Logan looked deeply into Gracie's eyes. Her eyes could melt chocolate.

Logan told Gracie, "I am here for you. I've always been here for you. Even in high school."

Gracie allowed a tear to trickle down her cheek. "You are right on one thing: it *is* high school all over again. I watched you walk away from me the day we graduated. I'm watching you walk away from me now. I'm not doing this again. I'm done. I'm over it, and I'm over you. Go ahead and leave, and go to the next hospital you've been assigned." The elevator doors opened, and Gracie ran out the hospital entrance.

Logan did not know what had happened to set these emotions into play, but he was going to find out. He replayed all of her statements in his mind. "Since high school" – when did Gracie ever give him the inclination that she wanted something more than their friendship. Had Logan missed the signs in high school? Logan knew at this moment, Gracie had feelings for him. He could tell by the way they made love the first time. He could tell by the way she looked at him when she didn't think he noticed.

Logan stopped. It hit him like a ton of bricks. He had never said the words to anyone. The words made a huge impact on anyone. Logan was in love with Gracie. In high school, he loved Gracie. He loved her heart. He loved the fact she always included everyone. Logan thought to himself, *I was too blind to see – I was in love with her then and am even more in love with her today.*

Logan needed to find Gracie. Gracie needed him, and in high school, he had been there. He needed to be there for Gracie today. Logan viewed the parking lot, to see if he could see Gracie walking. He could not. He walked outside into the parking lot. Gracie's car was nowhere in sight. Had she left that abruptly? Where had she gone? Logan went back in. He needed to find Anna.

When he got off the elevator onto the third floor, Logan immediately went to the nurse's station. He saw Anna. Anna was on the phone and held her finger up for the "one moment, I'll be right with you" signal. As Anna hung up, Logan could not get his words out quickly enough, and Anna cut him off. "She's gone home early, Logan. That was her on the telephone." Logan thanked Anna for the information. Logan could not leave. He had to finish his shift. He knew that as soon as the shift was complete and reviewed and had the final approval for the day, he was headed straight to Gracie's home.

As Logan was leaving the hospital and getting into his car, he could not help but revisit his thoughts about Gracie and how he felt about her. Since arriving at Pioneer Children's Hospital and seeing Gracie, his world had been turned upside down and inside out. All in a good way, because of Gracie. He looked forward to coming into work every day. He knew she would be there. Logan just could not admit that it was love when he first had "those" feelings when he saw Gracie.

What was he going to do? He had received his transfer papers to his next assignment. For the first time, Logan did not want to leave. In most cases, Logan enjoyed each and every new assignment. They were all learning experiences. He loved meeting new people. He loved traveling to new cities. He had made friends—albeit not close friends—all over the United States. Pioneer Children's Hospital was different. He didn't know why, but Pioneer had felt more like a permanent place. There was no way it was because of Gracie. He could not, would not admit that she was the reason for staying.

Logan began the drive home. He could not get Gracie off his mind. Without realizing or understanding, he took the direction towards her home. As Logan turned the corner that would place him on Gracie's street, he could see down the road. Gracie was not home. Her car was not in the driveway. Where had she gone? Logan was becoming concerned. This was not like Gracie. She had left the hospital. Gracie was dedicated. She would not have left the hospital if something had not happened.

Logan drove past Gracie's home and headed in the direction of his temporary housing, as travel nurses called it. He parked in his driveway, opened the car door, and walked to the steps. He pulled his keys out to unlock the front door. As he walked in, Logan looked around at his "temporary housing". In today's busy schedule of a travel nurse, Airbnbs were quite common. Nothing in this beautiful home was his.

The furniture, the appliances, the soft comforter, the blankets on the couch, the pictures on the wall – none of this belonged to Logan. If Logan could, he would typically travel home during the holidays, but if not, Logan would pack up his medical scrubs and casual clothing and belongings, and off he would fly to the next assignment.

Logan went to the refrigerator and looked inside. It was going to be a turkey and cheese sandwich kind of evening. He fixed his meal and grabbed a bag of chips off the kitchen counter. Logan grabbed a bottled water and sat on the couch to finish his meal. He did not even have the desire to turn on the television. He finished and cleaned the kitchen. As he sat down to check his cell phone for any messages, he remembered that Anna had given him her cell number. Logan decided to text Anna, just to check on Gracie. Logan sent the message and waited.

Anna turned to Gracie and said, "Logan just sent me a text message asking where and how you are. You cannot hide out forever. You are going to have to return to work, and you are going to have to face him, too."

Gracie knew Anna was right. At this moment, she could not go back to the hospital after the day's events. Plus, Logan would be leaving for his next assignment. Gracie nodded and said, "Yes, I know I'm going to have to do both of those things. Right now, though, I'm going to take a few extra days."

Anna knew that this was serious with Gracie. Very rarely did Gracie miss work or even ask for a day off. Anna pulled Gracie into a big hug and told Gracie, "You can hide out here for as long as you need."

Gracie chuckled. Anna really was her best friend. Unfortunately, Anna knew why Gracie was at Anna's home. Gracie knew as well. She was hiding out. She was hiding from the pain she had experienced today. She was hiding from the knowledge that he was going to be leaving.

Gracie pleaded with Anna not to respond to the text message. Anna did not listen. Anna said, "Just let me text him you are okay."

Gracie shook her head "no". She stated matter-of-factly, "Logan does not care about whether I am okay or not. If he did, he would have told me about the transfer."

"Fine," Anna said, "be hard-headed, be the difficult one. You can't see what is right in front of your eyes. When you do, it will be too late." Anna was done trying to convince Gracie of the obvious. Gracie was passionately in love with Logan.

As the day progressed, Gracie knew Logan would be leaving over the weekend. He had not told her directly, but Gracie had heard Anna and several other nurses talking about his next assignment and possibly throwing a little going away party.

Gracie was trying to convince herself she did not want to see Logan before he left. All the memories of standing at graduation and watching him leave came back to haunt her. It hurt then, and it hurt now. Now, though, the pain was unbearable. She felt an emptiness she had never felt before.

It was time for Anna to be home from her shift. Gracie saw Anna's car pull into the driveway and heard the door open. Anna walked in and saw Gracie on the couch. She flippantly commented, "Still haven't moved, huh?"

Gracie smirked and looked at Anna and said, "Nope." Anna sat down and hugged her. She told Gracie that Logan had left Pioneer Children's Hospital today. Logan had come to say goodbye to the nursing staff. Anna said he thanked everyone for their kindness and making him feel such a part of Pioneer Children's Hospital. And, then, he was gone.

The day was busy, Anna told Gracie. Some new patients had been moved onto the floors. Anna was tired. She told Gracie she was going to eat a sandwich and rest for a few hours.

Before she retired to the bedroom, Anna walked over to Gracie and hugged her tight and whispered, "It will all be okay." Gracie felt a tear trickle down her cheek and wiped it away. *Would it be okay?* Gracie questioned herself. *Why did Logan not tell me at the beginning that he was a travelling nurse?* A question Gracie would never know the answer to. Logan had left. It was too late.

As the Monday began, Gracie walked into the hospital corridors to begin the week. Two months had passed. Two very long months. Gracie wondered if he missed her, or if he even thought about her. Gracie could not bear to mention his name.

It would be time for the hospital's annual Christmas gala. This year's theme had been announced. It was Jingle and Mingle. Gracie loved Christmas. It was her favorite holiday. Anna was excited, so that made Gracie excited. Gracie had agreed to go shopping with Anna for a gown to wear to the event. Anna had told Gracie it would get her out of "that funk" she was in. So Gracie had agreed.

Saturday morning came, the day of the gala. It had crept upon Gracie rather quickly. Today, she and Anna were going to be pampered. Nails, toes, hair – "the works", as Anna liked to call it. When all was done and Gracie and Anna headed back home to dress, Gracie had to admit she was a bit excited to attend the gala. Gracie loved to see all the beautiful dresses that were being displayed.

Anna walked into the living room. "So, what do you think?" Anna inquired of Gracie. Gracie smiled and told her she looked exquisite. Anna then looked at Gracie and said, "You are going to surprise a lot of folks when you walk in tonight, Gracie." Gracie did not know what Anna meant. Gracie had chosen the perfect ivory petal cocktail dress. It was satin at the top, with a halter neckline and small rose petals outlining the bottom. The gown fit Gracie like a glove. Gracie felt confident in the gown. Tonight would be a night of new beginnings. Gracie had never worn anything such as this.

Anna and Gracie drove to the gala. Immediately, both looked at each other and said, "Valet, we are doing this right?" Gracie laughed. As the parking attendant approached and opened the door, Gracie placed one leg out, and he held his hand out to assist her. She smiled and thanked the young man. Anna had already stepped to the sidewalk, where she was waiting for Gracie.

Anna giggled. She told Gracie, "You just made that young man's night."

Gracie approached the elevator and pushed the up button. The doors opened, and both Anna and Gracie walked in. They inhaled the scent of Christmas. The lobby of the hotel was decorated in beautiful red and green and white wreaths, and there was one of the largest Christmas trees Gracie had ever seen. The lights shimmered and sparkled. The beautiful felt poinsettias were an added touch. Oh, yes, it was Christmas, and you could feel it.

When the doors of the elevator opened and Gracie and Anna exited, both heard their friends talking and laughing. Gracie and Anna took the liberty of joining their friends from the third floor of Pioneer. At the moment when Gracie walked up to the crowd, a hush fell over their friends, and all eyes were on Gracie. Gracie knew it as well. She had done nothing special. She was just in a cocktail dress. From the glances and stares she was receiving, she evidently needed to wear a cocktail dress more often.

The doors of the gala opened, and both Anna and Gracie proceeded to walk in. The room was breathtaking. From the centerpieces to the stage, everything had that Christmas spirit. They were assigned to a table. Anna found their number. As they were sitting down, Dr. Chrystmas approached them and wished their table a Merry Christmas. Gracie loved the fact that his last name was Chrystmas. It fit him. He was a very caring pediatric doctor—one of the best in the world. Gracie and the staff of Pioneer Children's Hospital had seen this first hand.

It was time for the dinner to be served. Gracie went to reach for her purse. She felt nothing. *Oh no!* she thought. *I left my clutch in the car.* Her cell phone and touch-up makeup were in there. She wanted to take pictures of the evening.

Gracie leaned over to Anna and said, I left my clutch in the car. I'll be right back."

Anna nodded her head and said, "Don't get lost now." "Plus, remember we did valet paking. Your keys are with them."

Gracie smiled and said, "I will be back, I promise."

As quickly as she could, Gracie left the dinner and headed towards the elevator. She pushed the down button. As she was waiting on the elevator to arrive, thoughts of him were in the back of her mind. Gracie wondered what he was doing. Did he celebrate Christmas with his family? Did he celebrate Christmas with friends? The doors opened. Gracie accidentally dropped her valet ticket. She picked the ticket up and walked onto the elevator without a second glance.

A rich, deep voice asked, "Which floor would you like, Gracie?"

Gracie's heart skipped a beat. It was NOT him. He could NOT be on this elevator. It was impossible. She was afraid to look up, for fear it was NOT him.

And then it happened. His hand moved to hit the "stop" button on the elevator. Gracie felt his finger touch her chin and turn it up, so she could see him. Gracie felt her legs were going to buckle. She could not breathe. She was going to pass out. There was not enough room in the elevator.

Gracie closed her eyes, for fear it was just her imagination. She heard Logan's voice, "Gracie open your eyes, look at me. It's me." Gracie opened her eyes. "I've missed you," Logan told her. "I looked for you the day I had to leave. I could not find you. Gracie, where did you go?"

Gracie looked directly into his eyes. "I couldn't, Logan," she said, "I just could not watch you leave for a second time."

Logan smiled and held Gracie's face and massaged the bottom of Gracie's lip, which had swollen with desire from his touch. "Gracie, I am back. I am not leaving you. When I left for my next assignment, I could not admit to myself that not only did I desire you, but I am in love with you. I love you, Gracie. You have my whole heart, my entire being."

Gracie looked at Logan. She had longed to hear these words in high school, and here he was, Logan Gere, telling Gracie he loved her. Gracie smiled. "I love you, too. I've been in love with you for a very long time."

Logan leaned in to kiss Gracie. He wanted of all Gracie's passion and love. He tugged at Gracie's lip to allow his tongue access to her sweetness.

Before they realized what was happening, the elevator alarm had gone off, and the door was opening. Both Logan and Gracie were surprised to see the entire third floor of their nursing unit smiling, cheering, and applauding. Gracie knew she was blushing. Logan was grinning sheepishly. Anna was smiling from ear to ear. Goodness, what a surprise. What a gala. What an evening.

Logan gently reached for Gracie's hand and closed his fingers tightly through hers. Gracie smiled to herself. So much for the makeup, phone and my clutch. She squeezed Logan's arm. Logan looked deep into her eyes and said, "Are you ready, Gracie? Because I am."

Gracie leaned her head on his shoulder and smiled. "I am ready. Lead the way." They stepped off the elevator with the promise of love and Two Degrees One Heart."

DE DE COX

Born and raised on a farm in Deatsville/Rooster Run, Kentucky, Deanna's grandparents had a lasting impression. This was the upbringing that brought forward the meaning of volunteering and helping your neighbors. Many memories were made with BeaBea, her grandmother who always made sure that if there was a need, the need was met. Buttered pies, hankies, socks and washcloths were always ready to find a home for church friends, neighbors and acquaintances. BeaBea exhibited kindness, caring and compassion – the Three Cs is what she called them. Even though, we all knew kindness did not begin with a "C", BeaBea assured Deanna that it did because BeaBea had captured her attention to inquire of the "C" and that's what was being done by volunteering and giving back to those less fortunate. BeaBea saw the need and instilled that need of empathy for others in Deanna.

Deanna grew up with a sister who had a way with words. She was the debater in the family, not Deanna. Her sister, at an early age, had an influence on the dream of becoming a romance writer. Many weekends, Deanna and her sister, would sit and read for hours and discuss how they would one day become romance writers. The discussions were intense and humorous. Deanna's sister is still her best friend. They work together and still share dreams.

As time marches on, Deanna married her best friend from high school. She proposed, because she knew he would not. He tells friends "Deanna caught me in a weak moment". The weak moment has turned into 34 years of marriage. Deanna has one child, a son. His heart is one of compassion. There is no greater joy than to receive the gift of life – a child for whom you have prayed for.

When the book became an idea, it was at an age when the stars were aligning. Deanna began writing at the age of 34. But the book took a backseat due to life and the birth of her son.

Life as it is now consists of a husband, a son, a one-eyed cat (rescue), a foster fail bulldog, adopted now, and another foster bulldog, full time job (with her sister, of course), volunteering and serving with many charities, pageants and NOW a romance writer.

Deanna has always been known as de de (the designated driver). And yes, it is spelled correctly. Of course, that is also to capture your attention. The 3Cs have played an important role in de de's life and continues. The memory of that conversation with BeaBea has never been forgotten and is being handed down to the future. The journey is but a step toward the path that God has opened. As you take the turns and twists, remember all those who have met you along the way and continue the journey.

CPSIA information can be obtained
at www.ICGtesting.com
Printed in the USA
BVHW031739240919
559278BV00001B/74/P